BEFORE THE LAST LIGHT FADES

"Sometimes The Greatest Magic is Believing in Yourself...and Others"

W & G COAKLEY

The Starberry Fantasy Adventure Series

Adventure One

ISBN: 979-8-9938493-0-0

W. G PUBLISHING

FIRST EDITION

PRINTED IN THE UNITED STATES

TRANSLATIONS: CONTACT US

AUDIO BOOK / ANIMATION SERIES 2026/2027

CONTACT: INFO@WGPUBLISHING.COM

To everyone who ever felt too small, too scared, too limited or too unqualified — you are exactly enough."

Remember

Every great journey begins with someone who is "too ... " taking one brave step into the unknown.

CONTENTS

First ancient map, provided to Morty by Ophelia. Old, worn and not complete. Is it accurate? Can it be trusted? Are there dangers that are not shown ? Morty will certainly need a better map.

Starberry tree, failing, dying.

CHAPTER ONE
THE DAY THE LIGHT WENT OUT

It was a Tuesday. The forest suddenly went dark, eerily dark. **Deep dark.**

Not the kind of dark when the sun goes down. This was much different. **This was 'wrong dark'.** The kind of darkness makes you want to quickly pull your blanket over your head and pretend the world doesn't exist. The kind of darkness makes every hair stand straight up and take notice.

It came on fast... like someone had thrown a thick, heavy blanket over the entire forest. All sound stopped. The air got an uneasy chill to it. Every creature seemed to be frozen in place, muscles locked, all thinking the same thing: *Something is very, very wrong.*

The glow-mushrooms grew on the tree trunks started dying. Their usual bright blue glow turned dim and sickly, like lanterns running out of oil. Fireflies struggled to keep their lights on, flickering on and off like dying flashlights. Even the moss lost its color, fading from brilliant green to dull gray.

And on the horizon, the Starberry Tree ... this massive, ancient tree had been glowing for three hundred years, so bright it made the stars jealous ... went almost completely dark. Just a few tiny lights were barely glowing... as to signal the end, but also the possibility of hope.

Now, you have to understand something. The Starberry Tree had *never* gone dark. Not once in living memory. Not in anyone's grandparents' memory. Not ever. The tree didn't just give light, though. It sang. Well, not exactly singing like we do. More like... humming. A gentle, wordless sound wrapped around you and made you feel safe. It was so constant, so normal, most animals didn't even notice it anymore. Like breathing. Like your own heartbeat.

But that morning? Silence.

Total, crushing, terrible silence.

And then came the voices... the '*whispers.*' They weren't loud screams ... they were worse. soft, desperate whispers somehow got inside your head and squeezed your heart. *Help us. Please, please help us. We're fading. We're dying.* The whispers had always been there, but they used to feel good ... comforting, safe. Now the wind carried those cries through the growing darkness, and every creature in Thistlewood knew: if something didn't change, this was the end.

Morty is a mole ... small, nervous, wore these thick quartz spectacles, always fogging up. He woke up Tuesday morning at 7:43 AM, which was twelve minutes late, and immediately started panicking about it. That was just Morty.

But this morning was different. Even before he opened his eyes, something felt off. His chest got tight. His paws started shaking. And when he pressed his paw against his favorite worry stone ... this smooth pebble he'd been carrying around for three years ... it felt cold. *Unfriendly.*

Then it hit him. The whispers were gone.

Morty sat up so fast he cracked his head on the tunnel ceiling. "Ow!" He grabbed his spectacles, shoved them on with trembling paws, and just sat there in his cozy underground home, listening. Nothing. Just silence where the tree's song should have been.

"It's fine," Morty whispered to himself, even though he knew it wasn't. "Probably just the wind. Or maybe I'm still dreaming."

But Morty knew better. He'd lived in these tunnels his entire life ... all eight years of it. He'd dug every chamber himself, organized every storage space, created the perfect safe little world where everything made sense. Taking a deep, shaky breath, he started climbing toward the surface.

When Morty finally poked his head out of his eastern entrance ... he had three different entrances, each optimally positioned for different times of day, because of course he did ... he saw it. The glow-mushrooms on the nearby oak tree were dying. The moss was turning gray. And in the distance, the Starberry Tree stood dark and silent. Fear hit him like a wave. His chest felt too tight. His paws wouldn't stop shaking.

Then he heard them ... those desperate cries coming from the direction of the tree. *Help us. Please. Before it's too late.*

Everything in Morty's brain was screaming at him to run back underground and hide. His burrow was safe. Organized. Made sense. He could just pretend he hadn't heard anything, right? But his paws started moving forward anyway. Because someone had to do something. Even if that someone was just a small, terrified mole with fogged-up glasses and a racing heart.

Meanwhile, about three hundred yards away and seventeen feet up in the trees, Sophie the squirrel woke up to her tail thumping against her nest.

Sophie's tail always knew when something was wrong before the rest of her figured it out. It was like having an alarm system attached to her butt ... kind of embarrassing, but occasionally useful.

She let out a big yawn, stretched her little limbs, and finally opened her eyes, all set to tackle the morning just like she always did ... with a ton of enthusiasm and an unwavering belief in her own greatness. Seriously, Sophie was the best. Best climber in Thistlewood Forest. Best jumper, hands down. You could probably call her the most athletic squirrel across six whole territories. Sure, she didn't exactly keep it a secret (alright, she kinda bragged about it all the time ...but who's really counting?). With a skip in her step, she made her way to the edge of her cozy hollow to take in the beauty of the forest.

And she she saw it.

The forest was dying. Mushrooms flickering. Fireflies struggling. And the Starberry Tree ... the massive, glowing, impossible-to-miss Starberry Tree ... was completely dark.

"That's... not good," Sophie said out loud. She talked to herself a lot when no one was around. " very, very not good."

The tree had been there her whole life. Constant. Reliable. She'd never even questioned it, the same way she'd never questioned gravity or trees or her own jumping ability. Now the forest felt hollow, like someone had scooped out its heart.

Then she heard the cries. Distant, desperate, heartbreaking. *Help us,* the voice said so faintly. *Help... Now ....Please.* The sound hit Sophie hard. It reminded her of when her little brother had called for help during a storm ... same desperate, scared tone. Sophie felt fierce protective urge kick in.

This wasn't just about a tree. This was about home. About family. About everything she cared about.

Sophie's mind started racing. She was good at solving problems, especially physical ones. This was just another challenge, right? A big one, sure, but still ... she'd never met a challenge she couldn't beat. She took a deep breath, fluffed her tail, and launched herself toward the center of the forest. Whatever was happening, she was going to help fix it. Even if she had no idea how.

And then there was Zip.

Zip was a firefly who was basically scared of everything and whose light had always been the weakest, dimmest glow in the entire forest. Zip woke up in the morning knowing something was wrong, but it wasn't unusual. Anxiety was kind of his default setting.

But today was different.

He opened his eyes and looked at his own glow. It was barely there ... just the faintest flicker, like a candle about to go out. "Oh no," Zip whispered. He flew to the opening of his hollow and looked out. Everything was darker. Dimmer. Even the other fireflies ... the ones with normal, healthy glows ... were struggling.

And the Starberry Tree's gentle song, the one that had always made Zip feel safe even when he was terrified of literally everything else, was gone. Zip looked toward the center of the forest and saw the tree standing there, completely dark.

See, the Starberry Tree was the only place Zip had ever felt like he belonged. When it was glowing with thousands of magical lights, nobody noticed how dim he was. There was so much light everywhere his little flicker didn't matter. He could just exist without feeling inadequate. But now the tree was dying, and his light was fading with it.

Then he heard the cries. *Help us. Dying. Please.*

Zip sat there on his little perch, wings trembling, thinking he should probably just hide. Because what he always did when things got scary. Hide. Stay safe. But then he thought: if the tree dies, there won't be any safe places left.

So Zip took three deep breaths ... like his mom had taught him to calm himself ... to make the scariest decision of his life. He was going to help. He spread his wings, checked very carefully for predators (because you can never be too careful), and flew toward the tree. His light flickered with terror the whole way.

By the time the sun was fully up, pretty much every animal in Thistlewood Forest had gathered under the dark Starberry Tree.

They came from everywhere ... families huddled, friends holding onto each other, even the animals who usually kept to themselves. Everyone stared up at this massive tree, it should have been glowing with thousands of magical starberries. The tree was *old*. Ancient. Its trunk was wider than a hundred moles standing paw-to-paw. Its branches spread out like a canopy over everything. For three hundred years, this tree had been the heart of the forest.

The cries were louder here, coming from deep inside the trunk. Not words exactly, but feelings pressed into everyone's mind: *Dying. Fading. Help us before it's too late.*

Morty stood near the base, adjusting his spectacles nervously. Sophie landed on a low branch with one of her perfect, graceful leaps. Her tail swished as she looked around. Zip flew in last, staying high and trying not to be noticed. The three of them didn't really know each other. They'd seen each other around the forest, sure ... Sophie was hard to miss, always showing off. Morty was a nervous mole who talked to himself about tunnel systems. Zip was... well, nobody really noticed Zip.

The crowd was getting loud. Animals calling out questions, panic rising like a tide. "What's happening?" "Why is the tree dark?" "What do we do?"

Then a voice cut through the noise.

"SILENCE !"

Everyone stopped. Because it was Ophelia, the ancient owl who was basically the wisest, oldest creature in the entire forest. She perched on a prominent branch, her moonlight-colored feathers looking somehow older today, more tired.

"Listen," Ophelia said, and her voice had a quality which made you pay attention. "What you're hearing ... those cries ... the tree's last warning. The Starberry Tree is dying. Its magic is running out."

A collective gasp rippled through the crowd.

"How long?" someone called out.

Days," Ophelia said heavily. "Maybe a week before the damage becomes permanent, and *before the last light fades* , forever.

"You could have heard a pin drop.

"But," Ophelia continued, and everyone leaned in, "there is hope. The old stories tell of a grove ... ancient starberry bushes grew before this tree even existed. They're hidden somewhere beyond the eastern ridge. If someone could find the grove and bring back even one berry, the tree could be healed."

For a moment, hope flickered through the crowd. Then reality set in.

"Where is this grove?" someone asked.

Ophelia's expression turned sad. "The knowledge was lost generations ago. What I know is this: it's somewhere past the eastern ridge. There will be trials ... tests to prove the seeker is worthy. And you have maybe a week." The hope started dying. Trials, tests, only a week? It didn't sound promising. It sounded impossible.

"Who would even try something like that?" a nervous rabbit asked.

Ophelia's ancient eyes swept across the crowd. "It would take someone brave. Someone determined. Willing to risk everything for the forest."

Silence. Long, heavy silence.

Then a small, shaky voice spoke up.

"I'll go."

Everyone turned to stare. It was Morty. Small, nervous Morty with his fogged-up spectacles and his satchel clutched like a lifeline.

"I'll go," Morty again, a little louder. "I'll find the grove. I can read maps. I've studied the old texts. I know how to navigate. And..." He swallowed hard. "Someone has to try."

The crowd just stared. A *mole*? A nervous, underground-dwelling mole was volunteering for a dangerous quest?

Before anyone could respond, another voice rang out.

"I'll go too."

Sophie dropped from her branch, landing perfectly in front of the crowd. Her tail was held high despite the fear churning in her chest. "I'm fast. I'm strong. I can climb anything and jump anywhere. If there are physical challenges, I can handle them." She glanced at Morty. "You handle the smart stuff, I'll handle the muscle. Deal?"

Morty pushed his spectacles up. "Deal."

Then a third voice ... tiny, barely audible ... joined in.

"Um... could there maybe be room for one more?"

A small, flickering light drifted forward from the crowd. Everyone turned to look. It was the tiniest firefly most of them had ever seen, and his glow was pathetically weak.

"I know I'm not brave or strong or smart," Zip said quietly, his voice trembling. "But the tree is the only place I've ever felt like I belonged. And I don't want to just hide and watch everything die because I was too scared to try. So... maybe I could help? I can fly. And see in the dark, sort of. And fit into small spaces..." He trailed off, his light flickering rapidly.

The crowd murmured skeptically. A firefly? One who could barely even glow?

Ophelia flew down to perch closer to the three volunteers. "Three *very* different animals," she quipped, and something that might have been a smile touched her beak. "A worrier, a warrior, and a... well, I suppose we'll find out what you are, little firefly."

She looked at each of them ... really looked at them ... with those ancient eyes which have seen centuries pass. "The old stories say the grove only reveals itself to those whose hearts are true. And looking at you three..." She paused. "I think you might just have a chance."

From somewhere in the crowd, a voice called out: "But they're so small!"

Ophelia's head swiveled toward the voice. "The mightiest rivers start as tiny streams. The tallest trees grow from the smallest seeds. Never underestimate small beginnings."

She pulled an old, yellowed map from a hollow in the tree and handed it to Morty. His paws trembled as he took it. "This is ancient," Ophelia explained. "Incomplete. But it shows the eastern territories as they were known long ago. It's the best guidance I can offer."

Morty unrolled it carefully, his eyes already scanning every detail, every marking, every notation.

"You'll leave at first light tomorrow," Ophelia continued. "Use tonight to prepare. Gather supplies. Say your goodbyes. Rest, if you can." She glanced at the darkening sky. "The journey ahead will test everything you are."

She looked at them one more time, these three unlikely heroes standing together. "The forest is counting on you," "But I believe in you. Sometimes the bravest heroes are the ones who are scared but do it anyway."

The crowd began to disperse slowly, animals murmuring about the strange trio, about whether they had any chance at all, about whether the forest was already doomed.

Morty, Sophie, and Zip stood there , not quite sure what to say to each other.

"So," Sophie finally broke the silence. "We should probably actually introduce ourselves. I'm Sophie. Best climber in Thistlewood. Also pretty good at basically everything physical."

"Morty," the mole replied, pushing up his spectacles. "Expert in tunnel navigation, map reading, and worrying about things. Lots of things."

They both looked at the tiny firefly.

"I'm Zip," he said in his small voice. "I'm scared of pretty much everything, my light barely works, and I honestly have no idea why I volunteered for this."

"Hey," Sophie said, her tail swishing. "Being scared and doing it anyway? Basically the definition of brave."

Zip's light flickered ... maybe with surprise, maybe with hope.

"We meet here at dawn," Morty said, all business now. "Bring whatever you think you'll need. But we leave at first light, no exceptions."

"Agreed," Sophie said.

"Okay," Zip whispered.

And so they went their separate ways, each heading home to prepare, to worry, to wonder what tomorrow would bring. The darkness settled in around them. It was time to get some rest. Tomorrow would come soon enough.

Morty and Sophie reviewing one of Morty's many maps.

CHAPTER TWO
PREPARING FOR THE UNKNOWN

After Ophelia gave them the quest, the three animals went their separate ways to prepare.

Each of them handled it... differently.

Morty had a problem.

Actually, Morty had seventeen problems, which he'd numbered and ranked by severity in his journal using a color-coded system he'd developed specifically for problem categorization. But the most pressing problem ... Problem

Number One, marked with three stars, underlined twice, and highlighted in red ... was this:

His tunnel was way too small for all the supplies he needed to bring.

"No, no, no," he muttered, staring at the enormous pile of equipment spread across his underground living room. The pile was now roughly the size of a small bear. "This won't do at all."

His home was exactly what you'd expect from a mole who alphabetized his emergency acorn supply. Every tunnel labeled. Every room with a specific purpose. Everything organized with a precision bordering on obsessive. His study alone had seventeen different maps organized by region, age, and reliability.

It was perfect. Organized. *Sensible.*

And currently, it looked like a tornado made of supplies had exploded in it.

Morty cleaned his spectacles and consulted his checklist. The checklist was four pages long. Single-spaced.

"Compass ... essential. Spare compass ... very essential. Emergency backup compass in case both primary compasses fail ... critically essential. Waterproof map case ... obviously necessary. Rope ... three different types because you never know which thickness you'll need. First aid supplies, sewing kit, extra spectacles, books on edible plants, books on poisonous plants..."

He looked at the pile. Then at his small travel satchel ... lovingly crafted from woven grass and tree bark, with seventeen different pockets because of course it had seventeen different pockets.

Then back at the pile.

The satchel was approximately one-seventeenth the size of the pile. Maybe less.

"*Focus, Mortimer,*" he commented sternly to himself, using his full name because he did that when he needed to be serious. "What is absolutely, completely, unquestionably essential?"

He stared at the pile for a long moment.

"Everything," he concluded. "Everything is essential."

He created a new system: Essential, Very Essential, Critically Essential, and "I'll Probably Regret Not Bringing This, but I literally cant't fit it." The last category was depressingly large. By the time he was done, his satchel was roughly the same size as he was.

"Perfect," he thought to himself, even though his paws were shaking. ..."Totally reasonable."

Meanwhile, three tunnels over and seventeen feet up, Sophie was having the opposite problem.

She wasn't bringing nearly enough stuff.

"Okay," she announced to her reflection in a small pool of water, "here's what I need for this quest: me, my incredible athletic ability, and my devastating good looks. Done. Perfect. Flawless plan."

Her home was in the high branches of an oak tree ... less of a "home" and more of a "collection of branches that Sophie sometimes slept on when she remembered to sleep." She didn't have much furniture. What she DID have was a collection of trophies from her various achievements, each with a story about Sophie doing something amazing.

She did a few quick stretches. "Should I bring anything? Food? Nah, we'll find food. Water? There are streams everywhere. Supplies? Supplies are what you bring when you're not confident in your abilities."

She did three backflips in a row and landed perfectly.

"When I come back with those starberries, everyone's going to lose their minds. They'll probably throw a parade. Maybe name a holiday after me. 'Sophie Day.' Has a nice ring to it."

A small voice in the back of her head suggested maybe she should bring *something*. Sophie ignored the voice. The voice was boring.

"Danger is just another word for fun," she told her reflection. "And I'm *excellent* at fun."

In his small hollow near the Starberry Tree, Zip was having a complete crisis.

"Okay, I'm going," Zip said firmly, tucking a tiny leaf-wrapped package into his travel bag ... which was actually just a folded leaf held with spider silk he'd collected very carefully from an ABANDONED web.

He flew in a small circle around his hollow, which was decorated with soft dandelion fluff and lit by his own dim glow. It was cozy. Safe. The kind of place where nothing scary ever happened.

"I'm definitely going. This is happening. I'm going to be brave and ... " He stopped mid-flight. "What am I thinking? I can't go on a dangerous quest! I got tangled in an empty spider web this morning!"

He landed on his favorite resting spot ... a soft piece of moss was exactly the right amount of squishy ... and put his head in his tiny hands.

"But the tree needs help," he whispered. "The whispers are gone. And maybe they'll need someone with a light?" He looked at his own glow, currently doing its usual struggling-nightlight-in-a-power-outage impression. "Who am I kidding? My light is pathetic."

He started unpacking his tiny bag. Then stopped.

"Oh, for the love of starlight, MAKE A DECISION, ZIP!"

He startled at his own voice. His light flared briefly with surprise, then dimmed back to normal.

Zip took several deep breaths ... it takes a lot of breaths to feel calm when your lungs are very small. "Okay. Here's what I know," in a loud voice because sometimes saying things out loud made them feel more real and less scary.

"The Starberry Tree is the only place I've ever felt like I belonged. If I don't at least TRY to help save it, I'll regret it forever. Even if I'm scared. Even if I'm useless. At least I'll know I tried."

His light flickered and pulsed ... still dim, still weak, but maybe just a tiny bit steadier.

"I'm going," he whispered. "This is terrifying and I'm going to be scared the entire time. But I'm going to do it anyway."

For Zip, this was the bravest thing he'd ever done.

Morty sat in his tunnel surrounded by supplies one last time. His satchel lay open in front of him, and around it were carefully organized piles of everything he might possibly need for a quest of unknown duration into unknown territory with unknown dangers.

He tried to sleep but couldn't. His mind kept spinning with all the things which could go wrong. Instead, he lit a candle and studied Ophelia's map, tracing possible routes, noting potential dangers, measuring distances.

Somewhere in his supplies was his grandmother's lucky pebble ... a smooth stone, had been in his family for generations. He held it for a moment, feeling its comforting weight.

If he was going to do this impossible thing, he'd be as prepared as he possibly could be. Even if preparation couldn't protect him from everything. Even if he was absolutely terrified.

Sophie spent her evening doing what she did best: climbing. She scaled the tallest trees in her territory, leaping between branches with reckless confidence, pushing herself harder and faster than usual. If this quest had physical challenges, she wanted to be *ready*.

But as the sun set and the forest grew darker ... darker than it should be, with the tree's magic fading ... Sophie sat on her favorite branch and stared out at the distant silhouette of the

Starberry Tree. And for the first time in a long time, she felt scared.

Not scared of the physical stuff. But what if that wasn't enough? What if the quest needed more than just athletic ability? What if she let everyone down?

"You can do this," she told herself firmly. "You're Sophie. You're amazing. This is just... a really big, really important challenge." Her tail swished uncertainly. "Okay, fine, I'm a little scared. But okay. Brave people get scared too. They just do the scary thing anyway."

Tomorrow, she'd prove she was as amazing as she always claimed to be.

Zip settled into his nest of dandelion fluff, his wings still trembling, his heart still racing. But tomorrow, he was going on an adventure.

For Zip, it was the bravest decision he'd ever made.

The next morning came cold and gray. The three unlikely heroes met at the base of the Starberry Tree, where Ophelia and a small crowd of well-wishers had gathered to see them off.

Morty arrived first, his enormous bag already weighing him down, his spectacles fogging up from nervous breathing. Sophie bounded up moments later, carrying almost nothing and practically vibrating with nervous energy. Zip flew in last, his dim light flickering with barely contained terror.

They looked at each other ... really looked at each other ... maybe for the first time. An anxious mole who'd spent most of his life underground, planning for every possible disaster. A confident squirrel who'd never faced anything she couldn't outrun, outclimb, or outjump. A terrified firefly who was certain this was the worst idea anyone had ever had.

Three complete strangers, about to attempt the impossible.

Ophelia stepped forward, her ancient eyes moving from one to the next. "You have everything you need?" she asked, though her gaze lingered on Sophie's distinct lack of supplies.

"Yes," Morty said, patting his satchel with confidence ... only slightly forced.

"Absolutely," Sophie confirmed.

"I think so?" Zip offered.

"Good." Ophelia paused, and for a moment she looked older than ancient ... like she was seeing not just three young animals, but something more. Something important. "The journey ahead will test you in ways you cannot imagine.

You'll face challenges requiring more than just strength or cleverness or courage alone."

She let the weight of those words settle.

"Your strongest tool isn't in any satchel. It's not physical ability or book knowledge or even bravery. Your strongest tool is each other. Trust in that. Especially when it's hard."

"We will," Sophie said with total confidence.

"Most likely," Morty added with moderate confidence.

"Hopefully," Zip whispered with basically no confidence at all.

Ophelia's voice cracked slightly, and suddenly she seemed less like an all-knowing ancient owl and more like someone who cared deeply about three foolish young animals about to walk into danger. She turned away for a moment, wings trembling. When she looked back, her eyes were wet.

"The tree welcomed me when I was young and alone," commenting quietly. "Fifty winters ago, when I had nowhere else to go. It gave me purpose. Home. The whispers sang me to sleep every night." Her voice steadied, but the emotion remained. "If it dies, I lose more than light. I lose the only family I've ever known."

The three heroes stood in stunned silence. They'd never heard Ophelia speak like this ... so raw, so vulnerable.

"We'll come back," Sophie promised, her voice fierce with conviction. "With the starberries. I guarantee it."

Ophelia pressed something into Morty's paw ... a small, smooth acorn. "For luck,"

Morty tucked it carefully into his satchel next to his grandmother's pebble. "Thank you. We'll do our best."

"Your best is all anyone can ask," Ophelia said softly, her ancient eyes warm.

The small crowd called out encouragements and good wishes as Sophie turned toward the eastern ridge, where the deep, dark, unknown forest waited. "Okay then," Sophie said, trying to sound confident even though her stomach was doing flips. *"Let's go save a tree. An* ***ancient*** *tree"*

Morty fell into step beside her, his oversized satchel bouncing with each step. Zip flew above them, his tiny light bobbing in the gray morning air like a fading star refusing to go out.

They walked into the morning mist, these three unlikely heroes ... leaving behind everything familiar and safe, heading toward the unknown. None of them knew what waited out there in the deep forest. None of them knew if they'd succeed, or even survive.

But they knew this: the Starberry Tree was dying. The forest was fading. And someone had to try.

Behind them, the ancient tree stood silent and dark, its branches empty of magic, its whispers silenced. Watching them go. Hoping these three small, scared, imperfect animals would somehow be enough.

The mist swallowed them slowly ... first their feet, then their bodies, until all remaining visible was Zip's tiny, flickering light.

And then even it disappeared into the gray.

Morty packed and almost ready to go...

CHAPTER THREE

Three Paths, One Disaster

They made it approximately forty-seven feet before the first fight.

"We should go this way," Morty announced, pointing to a well-worn path through gentle ferns and easy terrain. He'd already pulled out his map and was consulting it while walking, which seemed like a recipe for disaster but was apparently just how Morty operated now.

"That's the boring way," Sophie interrupted, pointing instead to a rocky hillside which looked significantly more vertical. "We should go THAT way. Much faster if you're not afraid of a little climbing."

"I'm not afraid of climbing. I'm being efficient."

"Efficient is just another word for slow and boring."

"Slow is just another word for thorough and alive!"

"Both of those routes look scary," Zip offered quietly from his position hovering between them. Neither of them heard him.

"My route is based on decades of tunnel-mapping experience and careful cartographic analysis!" Morty insisted.

"Your route is based on being too scared to take the interesting path!" Sophie shot back.

"I am NOT scared! I'm being REASONABLE!"

"Reasonable is BORING!"

"BOTH ROUTES LOOK SCARY!" Zip shouted, his light flaring so bright both of them actually stopped and turned to stare at him. He immediately dimmed and shrank back. "Sorry. I didn't mean to yell. I just... maybe we could find a route we all agree on? Instead of fighting? Because Ophelia said we should work together, and we've been on this quest for exactly two minutes and we're already arguing."

Morty and Sophie looked at each other. Then at their routes. Then back at each other.

"Your route IS kind of boring," Sophie admitted reluctantly.

"Your route IS kind of dangerous," Morty conceded with equal reluctance.

"What if," Zip suggested carefully, like he was defusing a bomb made of egos, "we took Morty's route today, since we're just starting out? But tomorrow we could try Sophie's more exciting routes?"

Morty considered this. "That's... actually very reasonable."

Sophie tilted her head. "And fair. I can live with fair."

"So we agree?" Zip asked hopefully.

"We agree," they said all at once.

They set off down Morty's route, walking in silence for approximately sixty-three seconds before the next argument started.

"We should keep a steady pace," Morty said, checking his pocket watch (because of course he'd brought a pocket watch). "Four miles per hour is optimal for long-distance travel while conserving energy."

"Four miles per hour is WALKING," Sophie said, already three steps ahead and looking bored. "We should be RUNNING. We could cut our travel time in half!"

"Running is exhausting and we need to conserve energy for emergencies! Walking is boring and takes FOREVER!" Morty countered. "We're maintaining optimal travel pace for maximum efficiency!"

"Optimal travel pace is another way of saying 'SO SLOW WE MIGHT AS WELL BE GOING BACKWARDS!'"

This time, they figured it out themselves. Sophie slowed down just enough. Morty sped up just enough. And without Zip having to mediate, they found a pace which worked ... walking for stretches, then jogging when the terrain allowed, then walking again when Morty's shorter legs needed a break (though he'd never admit it).

It actually worked. They were learning. Maybe not quickly, and definitely not gracefully, but they were learning.

They made it another two hundred feet before Morty stopped to consult his map.

"We're heading northeast toward the ridge archives," Morty explained, spreading his map on a convenient rock. "If we maintain our current heading for approximately ... "

"We can literally SEE the eastern ridge," Sophie interrupted, pointing at the ridge, very visible in the distance. "It's RIGHT THERE. We don't need the map."

"Proper navigation requires more than just pointing at things you can see!" Morty protested, but he was already folding up his map. "Fine. We'll use your method. But if we get lost ... "

"We won't get lost because the giant ridge is RIGHT THERE."

"Can we please not fight about maps?" Zip pleaded, his voice getting a strained quality it got when he was trying very hard not to panic. "Please? We just agreed on two things! We were doing so well!"

Morty tucked his map away with a sigh. Sophie stopped pointing triumphantly at the ridge.

"You're right," Morty said quietly. "I'm sorry. I just... I like having a plan. It makes me feel safer."

"And I like trusting my instincts," Sophie admitted. "It makes me feel more... me."

They stood in awkward silence for a moment. Then Sophie grinned. "Race you to the big oak tree?" And before Morty could protest racing wasn't part of optimal energy conservation, she was already bounding ahead, and Zip was laughing, and somehow Morty found himself hurrying after them, his satchel bouncing wildly, feeling something that might have been actual fun.

They stopped for lunch near a small stream, and this time the disagreement was about food.

"I brought enough provisions for seven days, carefully portioned for optimal nutrition and energy," Morty announced, pulling out neatly wrapped packages from his satchel. "We have nuts, dried berries, some cheese I traded for, and ... "

"You brought CHEESE?" Sophie interrupted, suddenly very interested. "On a journey where we're going to be outside in the heat for multiple days?"

"It's a special aged cheese , doesn't spoil easily. I researched it."

"You researched CHEESE?"

"I research everything!" Morty said defensively. Then he paused, looking at Sophie's distinct lack of supplies. "Wait. Did you bring any food?"

"I figured we'd just... find stuff. There are berries everywhere. And nuts grow on trees. Which I'm excellent at climbing, so..."

Morty stared at her. "You brought NO food?"

"I brought my winning personality!"

"Personality doesn't prevent starvation!" Morty took a deep breath, then another, then fixed his spectacles in a way he did when he was trying very hard to be patient. "Okay. Okay. This is fine. I brought extra supplies because I ALWAYS bring extra supplies precisely because I suspected something like this might happen."

"I brought a tiny piece of honeycomb," Zip offered, holding up something the size of a grain of rice. "But it's probably not enough to share."

Morty divided up his carefully portioned supplies without comment, but everyone noticed he gave Sophie a significantly larger portion than he took for himself.

"That's actually really thoughtful," Sophie said quietly. "In a judgmental, over-prepared kind of way."

"I'll take it," Morty said.

They ate in comfortable silence for a while, sitting by the stream, listening to the water and the birds and the general forest-being-alive sounds.

"We're not very good at this," Sophie said eventually.

"Not even a little bit," Morty agreed.

"We keep fighting," Zip added.

"We do," Sophie confirmed. "But we also keep... fixing it? Like, we fight, and then we figure out a solution, and then we're okay again?"

"That's called cooperation," Morty said, playing with his spectacles. "Messy, inefficient, frustrating cooperation. But cooperation nonetheless."

"Is it supposed to be this hard?" Zip asked.

"Probably," Sophie said. "If it was easy, anyone could do it. We're doing hard mode cooperation."

"I hate hard mode," Zip muttered, but his light was flickering in a way suggesting he might be smiling, ... if fireflies could smile.

They finished lunch, packed up (Morty insisting on properly storing everything, Sophie trying to just shove things in pockets, which didn't exist), and continued on their way. And for the rest of the afternoon, they did better.

Not perfect. Morty still wanted to stop and check his map every fifteen minutes. Sophie still wanted to take "shortcuts" which looked suspiciously like death traps. Zip still wanted to rest every time they saw anything even slightly frightening (which was often, because Zip found many things frightening, including but not limited to: loud birds, suspicious shadows, and one particularly aggressive butterfly).

But they were learning. Learning to listen to each other. Learning to compromise. Learning "my way or nothing" wasn't actually a sustainable approach to teamwork.

By the time the sun started sinking toward the trees, they'd covered about eight miles ... not as fast as Sophie wanted, not as carefully planned as Morty hoped, but solidly successful nonetheless.

"The archives should be just ahead," Morty announced, consulting his map one last time before the light got too dim. "According to my calculations, we'll reach them just after sunset."

"Perfect timing," Sophie said, and for once she didn't sound sarcastic. She sounded genuinely pleased. "We made good time today."

"We did," Morty agreed, looking surprised. "We actually... worked together pretty well."

"Eventually," Zip added. "After fighting about everything first."

"Details," Sophie said with a wave of her paw. "The important thing is we're here. We're together. We didn't kill each other."

"The day's not over yet," Morty pointed out.

"Always such an optimist."

"I prefer 'realist.'"

"Same thing when you're annoying about it."

But they were smiling. All three of them. Because despite the bickering, despite the disagreements, despite being three completely wrong animals for this quest ... they'd made it through day one together.

The entrance to the old archives appeared through the trees, exactly where Morty's map said it would be. A dark opening in the eastern ridge, covered in ivy and mystery and probably spiders (though nobody mentioned spiders out loud because Zip would panic).

"Ready?" Sophie asked.

"Ready," Morty confirmed.

"Ready," Zip lied, because he was absolutely not ready but was trying very hard to be brave.

They stood at the entrance, three friends who were just beginning to understand what friendship actually meant.

And then they stepped into the darkness. Scary dark!

One room in the Ancient Archives

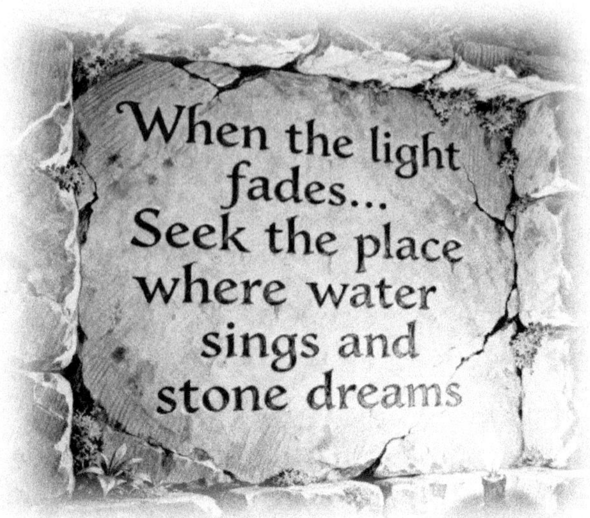

CHAPTER FOUR
The Archives

The darkness beyond the entrance swallowed them whole.

Morty fumbled in his satchel and pulled out a small lantern ... because of course he'd brought a lantern, along with seventeen other things they might possibly need. He lit it carefully, and warm light pushed back the shadows, revealing a tunnel stretching deep into the ridge.

"How far do these go?" Sophie asked, her voice echoing slightly off the stone walls.

"According to the map, the main archives chamber should be about a quarter-mile in," Morty replied, holding up his lantern to light the tunnel ahead. The glow cast dancing shadows on the stone walls making everything look like it was moving even when it wasn't.

They started walking, and immediately Morty's entire demeanor changed. His nervous energy shifted into something else ... fascination. Wonder. He ran his paw along the wall appreciatively, examining the craftsmanship with the kind of attention most animals reserved for looking at food.

"These tunnels are magnificent," he breathed. "Look at this stonework! The precision! The support beams carved from solid rock! And these ventilation shafts ... perfectly spaced for optimal air flow. Whoever built these understood tunnel architecture at a level which is practically extinct nowadays."

Sophie was significantly less enthusiastic. She kept looking up nervously at the ceiling, as if worried it might suddenly decide to introduce itself to the floor. Above-ground animals weren't meant to be underground. It felt wrong. Unnatural. Like being in a upside-down world, and inside-out at the same time.

"How are you so comfortable down here?" Sophie asked, watching Morty navigate the tunnels with the confidence of someone who was literally built for this.

"It's what moles do," Morty said simply, his paw trailing along the carved stone. "This is home. Or what home should feel like, anyway."

"It's dark and underground and there's probably no sky for miles," Sophie muttered, her tail twitching nervously.

"It's an architectural marvel!"

"It's a hole in the ground, Morty."

"A PRECISELY ENGINEERED hole in the ground!"

Zip flew between them, his small light adding to Morty's lantern and making the shadows dance even more enthusiastically. He'd been quieter than usual since entering the tunnels, his light dimmer ... not from fear exactly, but from the kind of overwhelmed feeling you get when you're in a place so different from everywhere you've ever been your brain needs extra processing time.

From somewhere ahead came a sound. Not quite a rumble, not quite a groan. Something in between made the small hairs on Sophie's tail stand up and made Zip's light flicker with alarm.

"What was that?" Zip whispered, his voice about three octaves higher than normal.

"Probably just the tunnel settling," Morty said, though his voice had gone up about half an octave too. "Stone does that sometimes. Shifts and settles. Completely normal."

"You're worried," Sophie observed, because she was getting pretty good at reading Morty's tells. The spectacle-adjusting was a dead giveaway.

"I'm cautious. There's a difference."

The sound came again, louder this time. Definitely closer.

"Maybe we should move a bit faster," Morty suggested, already picking up his pace.

They hurried through the tunnel, the rumbling sound following them like something large and stone-shaped was having a very slow chase scene. Just when Sophie was about to suggest they actually run, the passage opened up into a large chamber.

"The archives," Morty whispered, his earlier fear completely forgotten in the face of scholarly excitement.

The chamber was exactly as magnificent as the tunnels had suggested. Stone shelves carved directly into the walls, stretching up into shadows, even Morty's lantern and Zip's light couldn't quite reach. The air smelled ancient ... dust and stone and something else, something almost like cinnamon or old wood. Morty's sensitive mole nose twitched. This place had been sealed for decades, maybe centuries. Every breath tasted of history. Sophie's whiskers brushed against a shelf, reading vibrations in the stone. Solid. Old. Built to last forever.

The shelves were filled with scrolls and documents and ancient tablets, each one carefully positioned, each one potentially containing centuries of knowledge.

"It's actually kind of beautiful," Zip whispered, his light reflecting off crystals embedded in the stone walls, creating tiny galaxies of sparkle across every surface.

"It's full of dust and probably spiders," Sophie muttered, but even she sounded impressed. The chamber had a presence to it ... like walking into a library sleeping for centuries and was just now waking up to find it had visitors.

"We need to search for the map," Morty said, already moving toward the nearest shelves, his scholarly instincts overriding everything else. "Or clues about the Starberry grove. Anything which mentions starberries, ancient plantings, magical groves "

"That's like... all of these," Sophie said, looking at the literally hundreds ... maybe thousands ... of documents. "We'll be here for weeks."

"Then we'd better start searching."

So they searched.

Morty examined each document methodically, trying to decipher the ancient language the old ones had used. Some symbols he recognized from his studies. Others were completely foreign, like looking at alphabet soup and trying to find a recipe.

Sophie climbed the shelves ... because everything is climbable if you're a squirrel and you believe in yourself ... pulling down scrolls from high places and calling out what she could make of the titles. Which wasn't much, because ancient languages weren't exactly her specialty.

Zip flew from shelf to shelf, his small light illuminating dusty corners and forgotten documents, drawn to anything glowing or shimmering in the dim light.

"This one has a picture of a tree!" Sophie called from a particularly high shelf.

Morty's head shot up. "Bring it down!"

She carefully descended with the scroll tucked under her arm. They gathered around as Morty unrolled it, his paws trembling slightly with excitement. He studied the ancient text, his lips moving as he translated. His expression fell. "It's a record of tree plantings from two centuries ago. Interesting, but not what we need."

They kept searching.

"This one mentions magic!" Zip squeaked from across the chamber, hovering near a scroll glowing slightly in his light.

They rushed over. Morty examined it carefully, his eyes scanning the symbols. "It's a recipe for magical growth fertilizer made from crushed moonstone and singing nettle." He sighed. "Also not helpful."

More searching. More scrolls. More ancient documents containing fascinating information about everything except what they actually needed.

Sophie found records of water rights for the northern stream from before anyone living could remember. Morty discovered what appeared to be someone's very detailed grocery list from two hundred years ago ... apparently, ancient ones really liked mushrooms ... which made all three of them laugh despite their frustration, because somehow knowing that ancient magical beings also needed to remember to buy groceries made them seem more real. More like people ... or animals ... and less like myths.

"This is impossible," Sophie said finally, sitting down on a stone shelf and letting her tail droop with frustration. "There's too much stuff. We could search for years and never find what we need."

"We just need to be systematic," Morty insisted, though even he was starting to sound tired. "If we organize our search into quadrants and ... "

"Wait," Zip said suddenly, his small voice cutting through their discussion. "What's that?"

He was hovering near the back of the chamber, his tiny light focused on something carved into the stone wall itself. Unlike the scrolls and documents on the shelves, this was part of the wall ... permanent, unchanging, clearly meant to last forever.

Morty and Sophie hurried over, and all three of them stared at the carving.

It was a symbol: a tree with stars in its branches. The exact same symbol which marked the Starberry Tree on every map of Thistlewood Forest. And beneath it were more symbols ... ancient writing carved deep into the stone, the letters worn smooth by time but still legible.

"It's the old language," Morty breathed, his paws trembling slightly as he reached out to trace the carved letters. "The language of the ancient ones. The ones who planted the tree."

Zip flew closer, studying the carved images above the text. Figures ... animal-like but larger, more majestic ... stood beneath a glowing tree. "What were they?" Zip whispered. "The ancient ones?"

"No one knows for certain," Morty said, adjusting his spectacles. "Some say they were the first animals, blessed with magic. Others say they were something else entirely ...

guardians chosen by the forest itself. But they understood magic in ways we've forgotten."

He'd studied this language from books, dusty old volumes in forgotten corners of libraries. But seeing it here, carved by actual ancient hands ... or paws, or whatever the ancient ones had ... was overwhelming in a way he hadn't expected.

"Can you read it?" Sophie asked, leaning in close.

Morty squinted through his spectacles, his brain working overtime to translate the unfamiliar symbols. "Some of it. Let me see... 'When the light fades...'" He moved his paw along the carving slowly. "'...seek the place where water sings and stone dreams.'"

"Water sings?" Zip repeated, confused and slightly concerned. "How does water sing?"

"I don't know. Maybe it's metaphorical? Or maybe there's a place where water actually makes musical sounds somehow?" Morty continued tracing the symbols, his mind racing through everything he knew about the forest's geography. "And this circular marking here ... I think this is a map reference. A location marker. It's showing us where to go next."

"Where?" Sophie demanded, her tail swishing with renewed excitement.

Morty studied the carving intently, comparing the symbols to maps he'd memorized, to geographical features he knew, to everything his extensively educated mole brain could access. "I think... I think this is telling us to find a cave. A specific cave with water. Like a spring or underground river. Somewhere the water makes sounds ... 'sings,' according to this."

"The Singing Spring!" Sophie exclaimed, snapping her paws. "On the western edge of the forest! There's a waterfall there that makes musical sounds when the wind blows through it just right. Birds love it ... they go there to practice their songs!"

"Exactly!" Morty's eyes lit up behind his spectacles. "That's where we need to go next... where the next clue must be hidden."

For a moment, they all just stood there, staring at the ancient carving, feeling the weight of what they'd discovered. They'd found the first real clue. They had a direction. A destination. Actual progress.

"We should document this," Morty said, already pulling out his journal. "Make notes, sketch the symbols ... "

"Already ahead of you," Sophie said with a grin, watching him work.

Morty carefully copied the symbols into his journal, his paw moving with practiced precision. Each line, each curve, each marking ... all of it recorded for future reference. When he was satisfied he'd captured everything important, he closed the journal and tucked it safely back into his satchel.

"The Singing Spring," Zip said softly, testing the words. "How far is it?"

"About two miles west through the forest," Sophie said, already mentally mapping the route. "If we leave now and maintain a good pace, we could be there by late afternoon."

"Then what are we waiting for?" Morty asked, and there was something new in his voice. Not just nervousness or caution, but actual excitement. Actual hope.

They made their way back through the tunnels ... moving faster now, with purpose and direction and actual progress ... none of them noticing the way the carved symbols seemed to pulse faintly with light after they left. Just for a moment. Just a whisper of glow.

As if the ancient ones ... or the magic itself, or the tree dreaming in the distance ... approved of their progress.

When they finally emerged into open air, Sophie took the biggest breath she'd ever taken in her entire life and stretched dramatically toward the sky.

"Oh, thank goodness. I thought I was going to grow roots and become a mushroom down there."

"That's not how mushrooms work," Morty said, blinking in the bright light and adjusting his spectacles.

"You don't know my life, Morty."

Zip flew up into the open air, doing loops and spirals of pure joy. "Sky! Trees! And things that aren't underground! I missed you all so much!"

The forest stretched before them, the afternoon sun filtering through the canopy in golden shafts of light. Somewhere to the west, the Singing Spring was waiting with the next clue. And beyond ? ... hopefully, eventually ... the Starberry grove itself.

"Ready?" Sophie asked, turning to face her companions.

"Ready," Morty said, adjusting his satchel and pulling out his compass.

"Ready," Zip whispered, his light steady and sure.

The three unlikely heroes set off toward their next destination, each step taking them closer to saving the tree ... and closer to understanding what it truly meant to be a team.

CHAPTER FIVE
The Singing Spring

The journey west from the archives took them through dense forest gradually gaving way to rockier terrain. Sophie led the way through the canopy, leaping from branch to branch with her usual confidence ... though Morty noticed she was testing each landing more carefully than before. Learning, maybe. Or just being smart.

Morty followed on the ground, consulting his map periodically while Zip flew between them, providing a moving point of light in the lengthening afternoon shadows.

"How much farther?" Sophie called down from above.

"Should be just ahead," Morty replied, studying the landscape. "According to the map, the Singing Spring is in a rocky clearing where ... "

"I hear it!" Zip interrupted, his light flickering with excitement. "Listen!"

They all stopped and listened.

At first, it was just a whisper on the wind ... a sound which wasn't quite music but wasn't quite not-music either. As they moved closer, it grew clearer. Notes. Actual musical notes, like nature had decided to compose a song and was playing it on repeat for anyone who cared to listen.

The clearing opened before them, and there it was: the Singing Spring.

Water bubbled up from between ancient rocks, crystal-clear and cold, creating a small pool before flowing down over a series of stone ledges. As it fell, it hit the rocks at different angles, creating sounds ... actual musical sounds. Not quite notes, not quite chords, but something in between. The spray created tiny rainbows in the late afternoon light, and Zip's glow made them shimmer and dance.

"It's beautiful," Morty breathed, all his earlier nervousness about time and distance forgotten. This was magic ... not the flashy kind with lights and effects, but the quiet kind. The ancient kind.

"Yeah, yeah, very pretty," Sophie said, though even she looked impressed. "But where's the cave? The carving said something about stone dreaming, right? Where stone would dream behind the singing water?"

They spread out, searching the area around the spring. Zip flew close to the waterfall, his light reflecting off the surface in shimmering patterns. Sophie climbed the rocks, looking for anything cave-shaped or unusual. Morty examined the ground, looking for markers or symbols.

It was Zip who found it.

"Um, guys?" His voice was quiet but urgent. "I think I found something."

He was hovering near the base of the rocky outcropping where the water originated. Behind the waterfall itself ... barely visible through the curtain of falling water ... was a dark opening.

"A cave," Morty said, his voice full of wonder and slight dread. "Behind the waterfall. Of course! Where water 'sings' and where stone would 'dream' in the darkness!"

"We have to go through THAT?" Zip asked nervously, staring at the wall of falling water.

"We have to go through that," Morty confirmed, trying to sound confident.

Sophie was already leaping from rock to rock, finding the path leading closest to the waterfall's edge. "It's okay! There's a ledge! You can walk along it! Come on!" She paused at the waterfall's edge, took a deep breath, and jumped straight through the curtain of water.

For a heart-stopping moment, she disappeared completely. Then her voice echoed from the other side: "I'm okay! There's definitely a cave here! Come on!"

Morty went next, carefully picking his route across the rocks, testing each stepping stone. The spray from the waterfall was cold and shocking, making his fur stand on end and his spectacles fog up immediately. He paused at the edge, looking at the wall of water.

"This is a terrible idea," he muttered.

Then he closed his eyes and pushed through.

The water was like an icy wall ... shocking and overwhelming and very wet. His spectacles were immediately useless, just two circles of water-covered glass. For a moment, he couldn't see, couldn't breathe, could only feel the cold and the panic. But then he was through, on the other side, dripping wet but triumphant.

"I'm never doing that again," he gasped, wringing water from his fur.

"Zip, your turn!" Sophie called.

Zip hovered at the edge, the spray making his wings damp and heavy, his light flickering with nervousness. "You can do it, Zip!" Sophie encouraged. "Just fly straight through!"

Zip closed his eyes tight, took the deepest breath his tiny lungs could manage, and flew. The water hit him like a wall ... cold and shocking. His wings felt heavy. His light dimmed almost to nothing. For a terrifying second, he thought he was going to fall. But then he was through, on the other side, dripping and shivering but through.

"I did it!" he said, his voice filled with wonder. "I flew through a waterfall!"

"Of course you did," Sophie said, grinning at him. "You're part of the team."

They turned to look at the cave stretching before them into darkness, and all three of them stopped in wonder.

The cave was spectacular.

The walls sparkled with mineral deposits caught the light from Morty's lantern and Zip's glow, creating a magical effect where lights and shadows danced across every surface. It was like standing inside a geode, or what Zip imagined the inside of a star might look like. Water droplets clung to the crystals, each one reflecting light in tiny, perfect rainbows. The air smelled of clean stone and cold water. Morty's sensitive nose picked up mineral scents ... quartz, perhaps, and something metallic. Sophie's whiskers registered the cave's dimensions through subtle air currents and echoes.

"It's beautiful," Zip whispered, his voice full of awe.

"It's wet," Sophie observed, shaking water droplets from her tail, which was currently looking significantly less magnificent than usual. "And probably full of bats. Please tell me there aren't bats."

"Bats are actually quite harmless," Morty said absently, scanning the cave walls. "They eat insects and help with pollination ... "

"Morty. Are there bats in this cave? Yes or no."

"I don't see any?"

"That was a question, not an answer."

"Then: probably not?"

"I hate everything about this conversation."

They moved deeper into the cave, their footsteps echoing off the stone walls. The passage twisted and turned, sometimes narrowing so much Sophie had to squeeze through sideways, sometimes opening into chambers so large their lights couldn't reach the ceiling.

After several minutes of walking, the passage opened into the largest chamber yet.

And there, right in the center, sitting on a raised stone pedestal like it had been waiting for them for centuries, was exactly what they'd been looking for. A scroll under a glass dome looking like it had been crafted by expert hands long ago. And around the chamber, built into the floor and walls, were mechanisms ... levers and pulleys and pressure plates looked both complicated and vaguely ominous.

"That's it," Morty breathed, his eyes wide behind his spectacles. "That has to be the map. The map to the starberry grove."

Carved into the pedestal's base were more symbols in the old language. Morty rushed forward and began reading aloud. "'Three paths, three trials, three truths. Only together can the seekers claim what they seek. The high, the low, the light in shadow ... all must play their part.'"

"Three paths," Zip said softly, his light dimming with nervousness. "There are three of us."

Sure enough, three passages led away from the central chamber, branching off in different directions. Each one was marked with a symbol carved into the stone above its entrance: a tree reaching upward, a tunnel diving down, and a star shining in darkness.

"I think each of us has to take a different path," Morty said slowly, his brain piecing together the puzzle. He studied the mechanisms around the room. "Look ... these three levers are positioned so they have to be pulled at the same time. And those pressure plates are too far apart for one animal to trigger them all. Each path probably leads to a challenge. When we complete them, these mechanisms will release the map."

Sophie studied the three passages, her tail swishing thoughtfully. "Tree symbol is obviously me ... the high path. I'm the climber. Tunnel symbol is definitely you, Morty ... the low path, underground. And the star must be Zip ... the light in shadow."

"But what do we actually have to DO?" Zip asked, his voice trembling.

"Each path probably has its own challenge," Morty said, adjusting his spectacles and trying to sound more confident than he felt. "When we complete them, we pull our levers or trigger our mechanisms, and the map is released. We just have to trust we can each handle our own task."

There was a long pause. None of them liked the idea of splitting up. After spending the whole day learning to work as a team, being separated felt wrong. Scary.

"We can do this," Sophie said finally, trying to sound confident even though her tail was doing the twitchy thing meaning she was nervous.

"Before we go," Morty said, pulling out his pocket watch, "let's synchronize. We'll each take our path, complete our challenge, and trigger our mechanism. If we do it right, we should all finish around the same time. Agreed?"

"Agreed," Sophie said.

"Agreed," Zip whispered.

They stood there for a moment, the three of them, looking at each other. Just yesterday morning, they'd been strangers. Now they were about to face their first real test ... alone, but also with each other.

"Good luck," Morty said quietly.

"Be careful," Sophie added.

"We can do this," Zip said, and even though his voice shook, there was something solid underneath it. Something brave.

And then, taking deep breaths and trying not to think too hard about what might go wrong, they each entered their respective passages.

Sophie's Challenge: The Climb of Humility

Sophie's path led upward immediately ... stairs carved into living rock, spiraling up and up into darkness. Perfect. This was her territory. This was what she was good at.

The stairs eventually gave way to a tall, narrow chamber stretching up into shadows. The walls were covered in handholds and ledges, each one carved deliberately. And at the very top ... so high up Sophie had to strain to see it ... was a glowing crystal and a lever.

"Climb up, pull lever, save tree. Easy," Sophie said to herself, cracking her knuckles and rolling her shoulders.

She launched herself at the wall with confidence, leaping from handhold to handhold with the grace and speed which had made her the undisputed climbing champion of Thistlewood Forest. This was easy. This was fun. This was exactly what she'd been training for her entire life.

About halfway up, moving fast and feeling invincible, she reached for a solid looking handhold.

It crumbled under her weight.

For a terrifying moment, Sophie was falling. Her stomach dropped. Her tail flailed. Her brain went completely blank with pure panic. At the last possible second, her claws caught a lower ledge. But the momentum of her fall dragged her body against the rough stone wall. She felt a sharp, burning pain slash across her left leg as a jagged piece of rock tore through her fur and skin.

She gasped ... not from fear of falling, but from the sudden, shocking pain.

Sophie hung there, breathing hard, her heart hammering. Her leg was bleeding. Not terribly, but enough that she could feel warm blood matting her fur. The pain was sharp and immediate, demanding attention.

"SOPHIE!" Morty's voice echoed up from below. "SOPHIE, ARE YOU OKAY?!"

"I'm ... " Her voice came out shaky. "I'm okay! I just slipped!"

"YOU'RE BLEEDING!"

She looked down. Morty had somehow scrambled partway up the wall ... not far, but far enough to see her. His spectacles caught the light from above, and his face was tight with worry.

"It's just a scratch," Sophie called down, though the throbbing in her leg suggested otherwise.

"Can you climb down? Should I get help?"

Sophie looked up at the glowing crystal, still so far away. Then down at Morty, his small face full of concern. Then at her bleeding leg. Every instinct screamed at her to climb down. To get help. To admit she'd failed.

But something else made her pause.

"Talk me through it, Morty," she called down. "Tell me how to do this safely. Like you would."

There was a pause. Then Morty's voice came back, steadier now. "Test each handhold before you trust it! Three times! And plan your route three moves ahead!"

"Okay," Sophie said, taking a shaking breath. "Okay. I can do it"

"And Sophie?" Morty's voice was quieter now. "Slow down. There's no shame in being careful. Being careful is how you win."

Sophie felt something warm bloom in her chest despite the pain. "Thanks, Morty."

She climbed again. But this time, she tested each handhold exactly like Morty said. Planned her route three moves ahead. Moved slowly ... painfully, agonizingly slowly for someone who lived for speed. Her injured leg protested with every movement, but she gritted her teeth and kept going.

Each careful move felt wrong, unnatural. Every part of her wanted to rush, to leap, to trust her instincts. But she forced herself to be patient. To be more like Morty.

And slowly ... so, so slowly ... she made progress. One careful handhold at a time. Testing, planning, moving with deliberation instead of impulse.

When she finally reached the top and pulled the lever, her muscles were aching from the slow, controlled movements, her leg was throbbing with pain, and she was shaking with exhaustion. But also with something else. Pride. Different from her usual pride, which was about being the best and the fastest. This was pride in doing something the hard way. The right way.

And pride in having a friend who cared enough to help her, even from far below.

Somewhere in the walls, she heard gears grinding into motion. She'd done it.

Sophie carefully climbed back down ... still testing each hold, still being careful ... until she reached Morty, who immediately pulled supplies from his satchel. "Let me see," he said, his paws already working to clean the wound with antiseptic moss he'd packed. "This is deep. You're going to have a scar."

"A battle scar," Sophie said, wincing as he worked. “A scar to remember today by."

"To remember, being careful isn't the same as being cowardly," Morty said quietly, wrapping her leg with soft cloth. "And asking for help isn't weakness."

Sophie looked at this small, anxious mole who'd just talked her through the scariest moment of her life. "Thank you," she said simply. "For being here. For helping me."

Morty adjusted his spectacles, looking embarrassed but pleased. "That's what friends do."

Morty's Challenge: The Swim of Trust

Morty's tunnel led down, which was perfect because down was where moles belonged. The passage was smooth and well-constructed, with excellent engineering. This was going to be fine. This was his element.

The tunnel eventually opened into a chamber which made Morty's confidence evaporate instantly.

It was filled with water.

Not completely filled ... there was a narrow space between the water's surface and the ceiling, maybe six inches of air ... but filled enough so he'd have to swim through it to reach the other side, where he could see another glowing crystal and lever waiting.

Morty stared at the water with growing dread. He could swim. Technically. But Morty hated swimming with a passion usually reserved for forest fires. Swimming meant being out of control. It meant not being able to see where you were going. It meant water in your nose and ears and eyes and everywhere else water had no business being.

He stood at the water's edge for a long moment, his reflection staring back up at him, looking small and nervous and definitely not ready for this.

Could he go back? Find another way? No. This was his challenge. His friends were counting on him. He couldn't be the one who failed.

But he was so, so scared.

Morty thought about Zip ... tiny, anxious Zip ... who was afraid of literally everything but had still flown through the waterfall. Had still volunteered for this quest even though every part of him must have been screaming to stay home where it was safe.

Being brave doesn't mean not being scared. It means being scared and doing it anyway.

Morty took off his precious spectacles with trembling paws. Carefully placed them in his waterproof satchel along with his map and compass and pocket watch. He couldn't take them into the water ... they'd be ruined. He would have to do this blind. Literally blind. Without his spectacles, Morty could barely see his own paw in front of his face.

He took a deep breath, it shook going in and going out, and dove into the unknown depths of the water.

The cold hit him like a physical blow. Everything became dark and confusing immediately. His eyes were squeezed shut because the water stung, and even if they weren't shut, he couldn't see without his spectacles anyway. He swam forward ... or what he hoped was forward ... his paws paddling frantically, his lungs already starting to burn.

The space between the water and the ceiling was smaller than he'd thought. He had to tilt his head back to breathe, and even then, he barely got enough air before his nose dipped under again.

Panic set in, sharp and overwhelming. What if he got stuck? What if he ran out of air? What if ...

Then he remembered something. He was a mole. He could sense direction and distance underground. He didn't need his eyes. He had other senses. Other skills he was born with and honed over years of tunnel navigation.

Morty stopped panicking and started thinking. He could feel the current ... subtle, but there. Moving from where he'd entered toward the other side. He could sense the shape of the chamber around him, the same way he sensed tunnel dimensions when he was digging. The weight of the stone above, the flow of the water, the direction he needed to go.

He didn't need to see. He needed to trust himself. Trust the skills he'd spent his whole life developing. Trust his body knew what to do even when his mind was terrified.

Morty changed his course, swimming more efficiently now, using his natural abilities instead of fighting against them. The burning in his lungs got worse, but he kept going, following the current and his instincts and the subtle senses which made him a mole.

And then ... suddenly, wonderfully ... his paw touched stone. The far side. He'd made it.

Morty surfaced, gasping and shaking. His paws fumbled for his satchel, found his spectacles. In his panic and haste, his paw caught the frame wrong. He heard a small crack and felt one lens give slightly under the pressure.

When he finally got them on, he could see a thin fracture running through the left lens ... not enough to make them unusable, but enough so he'd always see the crack as a reminder of this very moment. A moment of trusting himself when he couldn't see.

The lever was right there. Waiting. He pulled it with shaking paws, and heard gears grinding somewhere in the walls.

He'd done it. Without seeing. Without planning. Without being able to control everything. He'd trusted himself, and it had been enough.

Zip's Challenge: The Maze of Darkness

Zip's star path led to a chamber, completely and utterly, absolutely dark.

Not regular dark. Not nighttime dark. This was darkness like Zip had never experienced ... thick and heavy and so complete even his small light couldn't penetrate it. The shadows seemed to swallow his glow the moment it left his body.

In the center of the chamber ... barely visible, just at the very edge of where his light gave up ... he could make out another crystal and lever. But between him and it was a maze of obstacles. Hanging vines swayed in air currents he couldn't see. Swinging pendulums appeared and disappeared into the blackness. Narrow passages between rock formations, he'd have to navigate without being able to see what was ahead.

Zip's first instinct was pure panic. Darkness was his biggest fear. Being a firefly with a dim light meant he'd spent his whole life feeling inadequate in the dark, unable to illuminate things the way his siblings could.

How could he navigate when he couldn't see? How could he avoid obstacles when he didn't know where they were?

His light flickered wildly as anxiety threatened to overwhelm him completely. He could feel panic rising in his chest, making it hard to breathe, making him want to fly back and tell his friends he couldn't do it ...

Then he realized something.

His light might not be bright enough to illuminate everything. But it was bright enough to see what was right in front of him. He didn't need to see the whole maze. He just needed to see the next step.

And he had other skills too. He could hear the whoosh of the pendulums swinging. He could feel the air currents around obstacles. His antennae could detect changes in the space around him.

Zip took a deep breath. What would Sophie say? Probably something about being brave. What would Morty say? Probably something about using available resources efficiently. What would Zip say to himself if he were being honest? I'm terrified. But I'm going to try anyway.

Zip flew forward slowly, carefully, his small light illuminating just the space immediately in front of him. When a pendulum swung toward him, he heard it coming ... a subtle whoosh of something large moving through air ... and dodged. When he reached a narrow passage, he felt the walls with his antennae and changed his course to fly through the center where it was widest.

Suddenly, his wing caught on something sharp ... a jagged edge of stone he hadn't seen ... and tore just slightly. The pain was immediate and sharp, but he pushed through it and kept going.

It was terrifying. Every moment, he expected to crash into something he hadn't seen, to get caught by something he hadn't heard, to fail in some spectacular way.

But he kept going. One small flight at a time. One careful dodge at a time. Trusting his senses. Trusting his instincts. Trusting himself.

His light flickered with fear and exhaustion, but it never went out. Small and dim as it was, it was enough. It was exactly enough.

And slowly, steadily, impossibly ... he made progress.

When he finally reached the crystal and lever at the center of the maze, Zip was shaking and exhausted, and his wing hurt from the tear. But he'd made it. Through the darkness. With only his small light and his own courage.

He pulled the lever with his tiny legs and heard gears grinding in response. **He'd done it.**

The Moment of Truth

Back in the central chamber, three mechanisms began activating at the same time.

Three levers pulled. Three challenges completed. Three friends discovering they might just be stronger than they'd known.

The grinding grew louder, gears interlocking, pulleys pulling, ancient mechanisms...waiting for decades ... maybe centuries ... for the right seekers to activate them. The glass dome over the map began to rise.

The three friends emerged from their passages at almost the exact same moment. All exhausted. All slightly traumatized. All completely and utterly triumphant.

For a moment, they just looked at each other.

Then, without a word, they rushed for a group hug ... or as close as a mole, a squirrel, and a firefly can manage, which involved a lot of squishing and some accidental tail-in-face moments but was perfect anyway.

"We did it!" Sophie exclaimed, her voice breaking slightly.

"We actually did it!" Morty agreed, his spectacles fogging up from emotion and also from still being slightly damp.

"*Together*," Zip added softly, his light glowing brighter and steadier than it ever had before.

And somehow a word meant more than all the others.

They approached the pedestal where the map waited, now accessible, the glass dome fully retracted. The map was drawn on parchment seemed to glow with its own inner light. It showed Thistlewood Forest in incredible detail, with markers and paths and landmarks none of them had ever seen on any other map.

And there, marked with a star, was a location deep in the southern woods. Beyond the Thornwood Thicket. Past the Swift River. Into the Deep Forest few animals ever visited.

"The starberry grove," Morty breathed, tracing the path with one damp paw. "It's real. And now we know exactly where it is."

"How far?" Sophie asked, already thinking ahead.

Morty studied the map carefully, calculating distances and terrain. "About five miles from here. Through the Thornwood Thicket, across the Swift River, and into the Deep Forest where the old trees grow."

"Sounds like an adventure," Sophie said, and despite everything they'd just been through, she was grinning. A real, genuine grin.

"Sounds scary," Zip admitted honestly. "But also... kind of exciting? Weird?"

"Not weird," Morty said firmly, carefully rolling up the map and tucking it into his satchel. "Its called being brave."

"I learned something in there," Sophie said quietly. "In my challenge. I've learned sometimes fast isn't best. Sometimes you have to slow down and be careful, even when everything in you wants to rush ahead."

"I learned to trust myself when I can't see the way forward," Morty added, adjusting his now-cracked spectacles. "I have skills and instincts that work even when I can't plan everything perfectly."

"I learned my small light is enough," Zip said, his glow pulsing with emotion. "I don't have to illuminate everything. Just the next step."

They stood in silence for a moment, each of them changed by what they'd just experienced.

"Ophelia was right," Sophie said finally. "We needed to work separately to learn to work as a team."

"The best truths rarely make sense," Morty said.

"Can we get out of this cave now?" Zip asked. "I love you both, but I really, really need to see the sky again."

They made their way back through the sparkling cave, through the waterfall curtain ... which was just as cold the second time but somehow less scary ... and out into the late afternoon sunshine.

The forest had never looked more beautiful. The trees had never seemed more alive. The sky had never been quite so perfectly blue.

"We're really doing this," Sophie said, looking toward the south where their next adventure waited. "We're really going to save the tree."

"all of us," Morty said, and it sounded like a promise.

"and me too," Zip agreed, the word carrying hope.

"a true Team" Sophie finished, her voice quiet with conviction.

As they set off toward the south, toward new challenges and unknown dangers and the mysterious starberry grove, they were different from what they'd been that morning. Sophie had learned patience. Morty had discovered trust. Zip had found courage.

The sun was sinking toward the horizon, painting the sky in shades of gold and orange and pink. They'd need to make camp soon. Tomorrow would bring the Thornwood Thicket and whatever challenges it held.

Sophie glanced back toward the cave one last time. Something about leaving the place felt unfinished. Like they'd disturbed something sleeping.

"*Do you guys feel that*?" Zip whispered, his light flickering.

"Feel what?" Morty asked, adjusting his cracked spectacles.

"I don't know. Like... like we're being watched."

They all stopped and looked around. The forest was quiet. Too quiet. No birds singing their evening songs. No rustling of small creatures settling in for the night. Just silence.

And in the silence, from somewhere far behind them ... back toward the cave, back toward the archives, back toward everything they'd just left ... came a sound.

Low. Rumbling. Like stone grinding against stone. Like something waking up.

"Probably just the cave settling," Morty said, but his voice had gone up half an octave. "Happens all the time with ancient structures."

"Right," Sophie agreed, though her tail had stopped swishing. "Nothing to worry about."

"Nothing at all," Zip added, flying a little closer to his friends.

They picked up their pace, heading south as the shadows grew longer and the forest grew darker.

None of them looked back again.

They didn't want to see if something was really following them.... *but was it?*

CHAPTER SIX
Growing Pains

They walked through the night, heading south toward the Thornwood Thicket. The unsettling feeling from the cave ... a sense of being watched, of something following ... had faded as they put miles between themselves and the Singing Spring. By dawn, they'd convinced themselves it had been nothing. Just nerves. Just the strangeness of ancient places.

By the time the sun was fully up, they'd convinced themselves of something else too: they were amazing.

They'd conquered the archives, survived the caves, completed the three trials. They were a team now. A proper, functional, successful team. Nothing could stop them.

That kind of thinking is dangerous.

Morty consulted his map while walking, not bothering to watch where he was going. He'd been doing that more often lately. Because he was confident now. Because he'd learned to trust himself in the underwater chamber, so obviously he didn't need to be quite so careful about everything anymore.

Sophie scoffed from her position in the trees above, doing an extra flip which was completely unnecessary. She'd been showing off more since the climbing challenge ... taking bigger risks, jumping gaps that were definitely too wide. "We should reach the thicket by sunset if you two weren't so slow."

"We're maintaining optimal travel pace," Morty said, not looking up from his map. "There's no need to rush."

"There's every need to rush! The tree is still dark, Morty. Every minute we waste is another minute the forest suffers." Sophie dropped down from the branches to walk beside him, her natural stride leaving Morty's shorter legs struggling to keep pace.

"We're not wasting minutes. We're being strategic."

"Strategic is just another word for slow."

Zip pointed out quietly, they'd had this argument before. He'd been quieter than usual since leaving the caves, his light dimmer, flying between them and trying to keep the peace like he always did.

Neither of them heard him.

The bickering continued. Back and forth, the same patterns they'd fallen into before, except sharper now. Meaner. Success had made them confident, and confidence had made them careless ... not with the quest, but with each other.

By the time they reached the Thornwood Thicket in late afternoon, they were barely speaking. The thicket rose before them like a wall ... a thick tangle of thorny bushes and twisted branches, which seemed specifically designed to make travelers miserable.

"We'll need to find the path through," Morty announced, pulling out his map. "According to my research, there should be a game trail ... "

"Or we could go around," Sophie interrupted, studying the thorny barrier.

"Around adds miles to our journey."

"Through adds hours of getting stabbed by thorns."

"The map shows a clear path ... "

"Your map can't show everything, Morty!"

The momentum of the argument is like a runaway cart. Maps versus instinct, planning versus action, Morty's careful way versus Sophie's confident leaps. Each exchange sharper than the last, each word cutting a little deeper.

"We should at least scout the perimeter before deciding," Morty insisted, adjusting his spectacles with agitation.

"That's just wasting more time! Time we don't have!" Sophie's tail lashed.

"Being careful isn't wasting time!"

"It is when you're so obsessed with your plans you can't see when someone else's way might actually work better! You can't handle it when you're not the smart one, the prepared one, the one with all the answers!"

Morty stopped walking so abruptly Sophie almost crashed into him. His paw went to his spectacles, adjusting them even though they didn't need adjusting. "I'm not obsessed with being smart. I'm trying to keep us safe."

"By making everything take three times as long?", responded Sophie

"By making sure we don't die!" quipped Morty

Sophie quickly replied, "We're not going to die from taking a risk, Morty!

Morty with sense of slight annoyance, “Your sense of direction told you to climb a cliff that almost killed you!"

The words hung in the air like poison. Sophie's face went pale ... she'd meant the swimming challenge, gotten it confused in her anger, but the damage was done.

"That was ME," she whispered.

"I'm the one who almost fell. I ... "

But Morty's hurt was already transforming into something sharp and defensive. "Right. Well. At least I'm not so desperate to be so impressive I'd risk everyone's lives just to prove I'm special. Maybe you should think about whether you're actually being brave or just being selfish. Whether you're trying to save the tree or just trying to be the hero everyone remembers."

Sophie's ears went flat against her head. "You think I'm selfish?"

"I think you brought basically nothing on this quest because you were too proud to admit you might need supplies. I think you constantly take risks without thinking about how it affects anyone else. So yeah, maybe a little selfish."

"And you're a coward!" The words exploded out of Sophie before she could stop them. "Too scared to do anything without seventeen backup plans! Too terrified of making a mistake to ever just TRUST yourself!"

Morty's face went very still. "Coward?" he said quietly. "You think I'm a coward?"

Sophie's anger drained away instantly, replaced by horror at what she'd just said. "Morty, I didn't mean ... "

But Morty's hurt had already sharpened into something cruel.

"Apparently swimming through that underwater chamber blind was cowardly. Navigating tunnels that kept us safe was cowardly. Planning so we didn't all die in preventable accidents was cowardly. Good to know."

"I'm sorry, I didn't mean it ... " Sophie offered her apology

"Caution without courage is just cowardice, right? Isn't that what you said? Well at least I'm not so desperate to be impressive that I ... "

"STOP IT!"

Zip's voice cracked through the air like thunder. His light was blazing now ... still not as bright as his siblings, but brighter than either Sophie or Morty had ever seen it. Bright with anger and hurt and something looking a lot like heartbreak.

"Just STOP IT! Both of you!" They turned to stare at him ... sweet, quiet, anxious Zip who never raised his voice, who always tried to make peace.

"You're both being awful! Both being selfish and mean! You're so focused on being RIGHT, you can't see you're destroying everything we built!"

Sophie tried to speak, but Zip cut her off. "No. I don't want to hear it. I'm tired of being the one who has to fix things every time you fight. Tired of being ignored until you need someone to tell you you're both being ridiculous." His voice cracked. "I'm just tired."

"We're all tired," Morty said, but his voice had lost its anger. Now he just sounded sad.

"No," Zip said quietly. "You two are tired. I'm done."

The words dropped like stones.

"What do you mean, done?" Sophie asked, her tail going very still.

Zip's explanation poured out ... he couldn't do this anymore, they clearly didn't need him, hadn't needed him to find the archives or complete the challenges, didn't listen when he tried to help, barely noticed him unless he was stopping them from killing each other. His light flickered and sputtered. "Tell me one thing I've contributed to this quest. One thing that actually mattered."

Silence. Not because there was nothing to say ... there was so much to say, so many moments where Zip had been essential ... but because both Sophie and Morty were too shocked and ashamed to find the words fast enough.

And the silence was exactly the wrong answer.

"Right," Zip said softly. "That's what I thought." He flew backward, away from Sophie's reaching paw. "I'm going home. You can figure out the Thornwood Thicket yourselves. Save the tree yourselves. You clearly don't need someone as small and useless as me slowing you down."

"Zip, you're not useless!" Morty exclaimed, finally finding his voice. "You're essential ... "

"I'm leaving."

And just like that, Zip flew away. Not in any particular direction. Just away. Into the darkening forest, his small light getting dimmer and dimmer until it disappeared completely into the shadows.

Sophie and Morty stood frozen, staring at the place where Zip had vanished.

"We have to go after him," Sophie said, her voice cracking.

"Which way did he go?" Morty looked around frantically. The forest was thick, and Zip's light was small, and he was already gone. "I don't... I can't..."

"Morty, what did we do?"

Morty sank down onto a fallen log, his paws trembling. He took off his spectacles and rubbed his eyes. When he spoke, his voice was very small. "We broke our team."

They searched until it was too dark to see. Sophie climbed every tree in a hundred-yard radius, calling Zip's name until her voice went hoarse. Morty checked every hollow, every burrow, every possible hiding place. Nothing. Zip was gone.

As full darkness fell, they made a miserable camp at the edge of the Thornwood Thicket. No fire ... they were too exhausted and too upset to gather wood. Just sitting in the dark wrapped in Morty's blankets, not talking.

Finally, Sophie broke the silence. "I called you a coward."

"I called you selfish," Morty replied quietly.

They both said it : "We're terrible."

More silence settled between them, heavy with regret.

"Zip was right about everything," Sophie said eventually. "We weren't listening to him. We were so busy fighting we didn't see he was hurting. We were making him feel exactly the way he was afraid of feeling ... small, useless, like he didn't matter."

Her tail drooped. "But he does matter. He matters so much. He was the reason we found the carving in the archives. The one who kept reminding us to work together." Her voice broke. "He's our friend. And we made him feel like he wasn't."

Morty adjusted his spectacles with shaking paws. "I get so focused on being right I forget to be kind."

"and I get so focused on being impressive I forget to be a good friend," Sophie added quietly.

They sat with the uncomfortable truth for a long moment.

"First thing tomorrow," Morty said finally, "before we even think about the thicket or the grove or the tree, we find Zip. And we apologize. Really apologize."

"Not just 'sorry you're upset,'" Sophie agreed. "Sorry we were awful."

"We have to mean it."

"We do mean it."

But how do you find one tiny firefly in an enormous forest when he doesn't want to be found?

They didn't sleep. Every sound made them jump, hoping it was Zip coming back. Every distant light made their hearts leap before crushing disappointment set in.

Around midnight, Sophie heard it. The whisper. So faint she almost thought she'd imagined it ... a sound that wasn't quite a voice, words that weren't quite words, the kind of sound the Starberry Tree used to make before it went dark.

She sat up, listening hard. The whisper came again, slightly louder, seeming to suggest a direction. West. Toward the deeper part of the forest.

She shook Morty awake. "I think I heard something."

Morty sat up instantly, cleaning his spectacles. "Zip?"

"No. The whispers. The tree's whispers, or something like them."

Morty paused, listening. There ... so soft he'd almost missed it, but definitely there. A whisper that felt like guidance, like hope. "West," he said.

"West," Sophie agreed.

They didn't discuss it. They just walked. Through the dark forest, guided by whispers and desperation. They pushed through underbrush, stumbled over roots, followed something they couldn't quite see or hear but could definitely feel.

And then, in a small clearing beneath an ancient oak tree, they saw it. A tiny light. Dim and flickering. Moving in small, aimless circles.

"Zip," Sophie breathed.

They ran across the clearing. Zip heard them coming and tried to fly away, but Sophie was faster. She leaped, caught a low branch, swung herself up, and positioned herself directly in his path.

"Please don't go," she said. "Please. Just let us talk. And if you still want to leave after, we won't stop you. We promise."

Zip hovered uncertainly, his light flickering with fear and hurt and maybe ... just maybe ... a tiny bit of hope. "Why should I listen? You two made it pretty clear you don't need me."

Morty arrived at the base of the tree, looking up at them both. "We made it clear we're idiots. We're selfish and thoughtless and completely blind to what's actually important."

"We were wrong," Sophie added. "So wrong about everything."

"What thing?" Zip asked warily.

"That you're not just part of this team. You ARE the team," Sophie said softly. "You're the heart of everything we've done. The reason we found the clues. The reason we haven't killed each other."

"I'm the referee," Zip said bitterly. "The mediator."

"No," Morty shook his head firmly. "You're the one who sees what we're too blind to see. You found the carving in the archives when we missed it completely. You completed a challenge in total darkness that would have destroyed either of us. You're the one who reminds us what actually matters when we get lost in our own egos."

"You're the bravest one here," Sophie said. "Because you're scared of everything and you do it anyway. Because you speak up even when you're terrified of conflict. Because you left when we were treating you badly ... which took more courage than anything Morty or I have done."

Zip's light dimmed with uncertainty. "You really think that?"

"We know *that*," they both said.

Silence. Zip flew in a small circle, his light pulsing with emotion. When he finally spoke, his voice was raw. "You hurt me. Both of you. You made me feel exactly the way I was afraid of feeling. Small. Useless. Like my tiny light doesn't matter."

"We know," Sophie whispered. "And we're so, so sorry."

"We can't promise we won't fight again," Morty admitted. "We probably will. We're both stubborn. But we can promise to listen to you. Actually listen. And we can promise to remember what's actually important ... not being right, not being impressive, but being a team. Being friends."

"Being family," Sophie added quietly.

Zip's light flared brighter. "Family?"

"If you'll have us," Sophie said. "Even though we're the worst and we don't deserve it."

Zip flew another circle, slower this time, thinking. And then, so quietly they almost missed it: "I don't want to go home."

Hope bloomed in Sophie's chest. "You don't?"

"I want to save the tree. It's my safe place. My special place. And I want to save it with my friends." His voice grew stronger. "Even when they're being idiots."

"We're definitely idiots," Morty agreed.

"Absolutely the biggest idiots," Sophie confirmed.

Zip's light glowed warm and steady. "But you're my idiots. And I guess I'm not ready to give up on you yet."

"Can we start over? From right now? Be better?" Sophie asked.

"We can try," Zip said. Then, more firmly: "We will."

He flew down, and the three of them came embraced in another group hug. This one was tighter than the last, more desperate, more precious because they'd almost lost it.

"I'm sorry I called you a coward," Sophie whispered to Morty. "You're the bravest mole I know."

"I'm sorry I called you selfish," Morty whispered back. "You're the most generous squirrel I know. You just show it differently than I expected."

Together, they turned to Zip. "We're sorry we made you feel small. Your light is perfect. You're perfect. We're so lucky you're here."

Zip's light blazed ... still not as bright as his siblings, still dim by firefly standards, but brighter than it had ever been. Because it wasn't just his light anymore. It was their light.

They held each other in the small clearing beneath the ancient oak, guided there by whispers they couldn't quite explain, held together by something stronger than magic.

"So," Zip said eventually, his voice only slightly wobbly. "What do we do now?"

Morty adjusted his spectacles. "Now we tackle the Thornwood Thicket."

They walked back to their camp as the first hints of dawn began painting the sky. None of them mentioned the whispers guiding them. Some things were too magical to question.

Tomorrow they'd face the thorns and continue their quest. But tonight ... this early morning ... they'd learned something more valuable than any map or skill. They'd learned the hardest part of friendship isn't the adventures or the challenges.

It's admitting when you're wrong. It's apologizing when you've hurt someone. It's choosing to be better even when being better is hard.

They'd broken their team. And then ... painfully, honestly, imperfectly ... they'd built it back stronger than before.

A nervous, self-doubting firefly with a gentle heart who constantly worries he's not bright enough... can he help the team ?

CHAPTER SEVEN
The Grove

They slept until mid-morning, exhausted from the night's search and reconciliation. When they finally woke, the world felt different. Lighter. Like the forest itself approved of what they'd rebuilt.

Morning sun filtered through the leaves as they gathered for breakfast ... berries and nuts from Morty's perfectly organized supplies. They were having breakfast at the edge of the Thornwood Thicket, ready to face it together.

"According to this, there IS a path through the thicket," Morty said, spreading his map out on a flat rock. "It's narrow and winds around a lot, but it exists."

Sophie peered over his shoulder. "How narrow are we talking?"

"Single file narrow. And watch-out-for-thorns narrow. Lots and lots of thorns."

Zip looked up from his honeycomb, his light back to steady this morning ... dim but content. "Sounds absolutely delightful. Like a nightmare obstacle course designed by someone who really hates fun."

Sophie blinked at him. "That's... oddly specific."

"I've had time to think about my fears. I've categorized them by probability and severity. Nightmare obstacle courses fall somewhere between 'getting stuck in a spider web' and 'being eaten by a bird.'"

Morty looked up from his map with actual respect. "You categorized your fears?"

"Of course. Doesn't everyone?" Zip shrugged his tiny shoulders. "I've been spending time with you. Some of the organization rubbed off. I now have a mental filing system for my anxieties. Very efficient."

Morty looked genuinely touched. "That's the nicest thing anyone has ever said about my influence."

"I've also learned some recklessness from Sophie," Zip added. "Yesterday when I left, I just flew off without any plan whatsoever. Normally, I would've spent three hours deciding which direction to go and then been too scared to actually leave."

Sophie winced. "I'm... not sure if I should be proud or apologetic ."

"Both," Zip said firmly. "Definitely both."

They packed up camp differently this time. Sophie didn't rush ahead. Morty didn't over-plan every detail. Zip actually spoke up when he had ideas. They finally figured out how they fit.

The entrance to the path was exactly where Morty's map said it would be ... a narrow gap between two massive thornbushes looked personally offended by the concept of travelers.

"Right," Sophie said, eyeing the path ahead. It twisted through thorny branches so thick you could barely see three feet in front of you. "Who goes first?"

They sorted it out quickly: Morty would lead since he was lowest to the ground and better for spotting obstacles. Zip would take the middle, where his light could help Morty see and he could fly up to scout if needed. Sophie would go last, able to climb up for a view ahead and watch their backs.

They looked at each other and smiled. No fighting. No arguing. Just teamwork.

"Let's do this," Morty said, adjusting his spectacles.

The Thornwood Thicket was exactly as terrible as it looked.

The path twisted like an anxious snake ... left, right, sometimes looping back on itself for no reason. Thorns reached out from every direction like they had personal grudges. The air was thick and close, smelling of earth and growing things and something old and wild and just slightly magical.

"Thorn ambush at two o'clock!" Morty called out from the front, and the others adjusted accordingly. When the path got too dark, Zip flew ahead to light the way. When it got too confusing to navigate, Sophie would carefully ... very carefully, with much complaining ... shimmy up a thornbush to get a view from above.

Sophie muttered as thorns caught her tail for maybe the seventeenth time. "I'm going to have nightmares about thorns for the rest of my life."

"At least you'll have company," Zip said, helping her untangle. "I'll be having the same nightmares."

After about an hour of thorny misery, they stopped in a slightly wider section of path. Sophie picked thorns out of her tail while Morty checked his map.

"Maybe another hour," Morty estimated. "The path should widen soon. Then the Swift River. Then the Deep Forest. Then the grove."

They sat there for a moment, feeling the weight of how close they were.

"Do you think the starberries will actually work?" Zip asked, his voice small and uncertain. "Do you think we can really save the tree?"

"We have to," Morty said firmly. "We've come too far to fail now."

Before Zip could spiral into what-ifs, Sophie interrupted gently. "Don't spiral. Just focus on the next step. Someone very smart told us that once."

Zip's light sparked with surprise. "I said that?"

"You did," Sophie confirmed. "And it was exactly what we needed to hear."

"Oh." Zip's voice got even smaller. "I guess I'm smarter than I thought."

"You're the smartest," Morty and Sophie said.

They kept going. And the path did widen, just like Morty's map promised. The thorns got less aggressive. And finally ... wonderfully, beautifully, miraculously ... they stumbled out of the Thornwood Thicket into open forest.

All three of them just stopped and breathed.

"We did it without fighting once," Sophie said, amazed.

"Without panicking," Zip added proudly. "Well, I panicked internally, but I didn't fly away or make it everyone else's problem."

They looked at each other and laughed. Pure, genuine, we're-actually-good-at-this-now laughter.

"Morty threatened to 'organize the thornbush into next week,'" Zip pointed out. "Which was confusing but seemed aggressive."

"The thornbush knew what it did," Morty said darkly.

Ahead of them, they could hear water. The Swift River, rushing over rocks. According to the map, they'd need to cross it to reach the Deep Forest.

The river was swift, all right. Fast and cold and significantly more dangerous than any of them had hoped.

"Well," Sophie said, staring at the churning water. "unfortunate."

Morty studied his map, looking for a crossing point. "There ... upstream. 'The Old Crossing.'"

They found it: an ancient log, worn smooth by water and time, stretching from one bank to the other. It was narrow, looked slippery, and the water below moved fast enough that falling in would be very bad.

"I'll go first," Sophie volunteered. "I'm best at balance."

"Are you sure?" Morty asked, concerned.

"I'm sure. I'll cross, then help guide you from the other side."

Sophie stepped onto the log with no showing off this time, no extra flips. Just steady concentration. The log was slippery and shifted under her weight. Halfway across, she slipped. For one heart-stopping moment, she teetered on the edge, arms windmilling, tail whipping for balance.

"SOPHIE!" Zip shrieked.

But she caught herself. Steadied. Took a breath and kept going. When she reached the other side, her grin was only slightly shaky. "See? Easy!"

"That was the opposite of easy!" Zip called back.

Sophie coached Morty across next, talking him through each careful step. He tested his weight multiple times before committing, and his paws were shaking when he finally reached the other side. But he made it.

Then it was Zip's turn. He hovered at the river's edge, his light flickering nervously. "Can't I just fly across?"

"It's pretty windy over the water," Morty observed. "You might get blown off course."

Right on cue, a gust whipped through, making branches sway and sending leaves spiraling into the river.

"Oh," Zip said in a very small voice. "Right."

"You flew through a waterfall," Sophie encouraged. "You navigated a maze in total darkness. This is just a log."

"A very narrow, very slippery log over a very dangerous river," Zip pointed out.

"But you have wings," Morty said. "If you start to fall, you can fly. You have an advantage neither of us had."

Zip considered this, his light pulsing. "hmmm, that's actually a good point."

"I have them occasionally," Morty said with dignity.

Zip took the deepest breath his tiny lungs could manage and started across. He didn't walk ... his legs were too short, the log too slippery. Instead, he flew just above the surface, following the log's path, using it as a guide.

Halfway across, a gust of wind hit him. His wings struggled, his light flickered wildly. Sophie and Morty shouted his name. But Zip fought it, wings beating frantically. His light blazed brighter than it ever had in daylight ... still not as bright as his siblings, but bright enough. Strong enough. Exactly enough.

He made it across and collapsed on the bank, breathing hard.

"Can we please stop practicing the 'almost dying' skill?" Morty asked, his voice shaky.

"Agreed," Sophie and Zip said agreeingly.

They followed the map deeper into the forest, and the trees started to change. These weren't normal Thistlewood trees. These were old. Ancient. Trunks so wide you couldn't see around them. Branches disappearing into a canopy so thick the light filtering through was green and gold and felt like time itself.

The Deep Forest.

Sophie felt the difference in her paws ... bark rougher and thicker, covered in moss cushioning every step. The branches above creaked in ways normal trees didn't, like they were speaking to each other in groans and sighs.

Morty's underground senses told him the earth here was different too. The roots went down deep. Way deeper than any roots should go, into layers of soil that had been there since before anyone could remember.

"It feels different here," Zip whispered.

"It feels like we're being watched," Sophie added.

"Not in a bad way, though," Morty said thoughtfully. "More like... observed. Evaluated."

The whispers started then. Soft and gentle, like leaves rustling, like water singing, like starlight would sound if starlight had a voice. Coming from everywhere and nowhere at once.

This way, the whispers seemed to say. Or maybe they were just a feeling. A direction. *This way, little ones. You're close now. So close.*

None of them questioned it. After everything, magic whispers seemed perfectly reasonable. They followed the feeling through the ancient trees, over soft moss, past mushrooms glowing faintly in the shadows.

And then ... quite suddenly ... they were there.

The clearing opened before them like a secret being revealed. In its center, surrounded by ancient stones and bathed in the last light of the setting sun, was the starberry grove.

Seven bushes, each one no taller than Sophie. Leaves shimmering silver-green. Branches humming with magic. And on those branches, glowing softly in the dimming light ... starberries. They looked exactly like their name: small, round fruits glowing from within, like someone had captured starlight and shaped it into berries. Some glowed silver, some gold, some glowed colors that didn't quite have names.

"It's real," Morty breathed. "It's actually, really, truly real."

"It's beautiful," Zip whispered.

"It's perfect," Sophie added.

They moved forward, drawn toward the grove ... and stopped dead when a massive shadow rose from behind the largest stone.

A bear. Not just any bear. The biggest bear any of them had ever seen, with dark fur graying at the muzzle and eyes looking ancient and knowing and not particularly pleased to see visitors.

"Well," the bear rumbled, his voice like rocks grinding. "Look what stumbled into my grove."

Sophie's tail poofed to three times its normal size. Morty's paw went to his spectacles. Zip's light flickered between bright and dim like it couldn't decide whether to glow with fear or hide in darkness.

The bear studied them with those ancient eyes, taking his time. Then, quite deliberately ... slowly enough they could see exactly what he was doing ... he moved to stand between them and the starberry bushes.

"**I am Thornback,**" the bear said with an ancient, commanding authority.

THORNBACK... the guardian of the starberries

"Guardian of this grove for forty winters. Born beneath the Starberry Tree when it was young and I was younger." He leaned down until his massive head was level with them, close enough they could feel the warmth of his breath. It smelled like honey and earth and something wild they couldn't name.

"And I have three questions for three small creatures who come seeking magic that is not theirs."

The air felt heavy. Waiting.

"First question: Why are you here?"

Sophie found her voice first, though it came out higher than usual. "The Starberry Tree went dark. The forest is suffering. We came to get starberries to save it. To bring the light back."

"Second question." Thornback continued like she hadn't even spoken, like her answer was just air passing through the grove. "What gives you the right?"

Morty pushed his spectacles with trembling paws. "We don't know if we have the right. But we have the need. The forest is suffering. The tree is our home. We had to try."

"Third question." His voice got quieter, which somehow made it more intimidating. "Are you worthy?"

Silence fell over the grove like a blanket. None of them knew how to answer that.

"How..." Zip's voice was barely audible. "How do we prove we're worthy?"

Thornback settled back on his haunches, looking at them thoughtfully. "You don't prove. You tell. Tell me your story. Tell me how three small creatures ... a mole, a squirrel, and a firefly ... came to be standing in my grove at sunset asking for magic."

"Tell you everything ??" Morty asked.

"Everything that matters."

They looked at each other ... a whole conversation happening in one glance.

"I'll start," Sophie said.

She sat down on the moss, Morty and Zip settling beside her, while Thornback remained standing, looming and massive, but listening.

"Three days ago, I woke up and the tree was dark. I was angry because the tree was special and someone needed to fix it. I thought I was going to be the hero. Save the day alone. Be impressive. Have everyone remember my name." She took a breath. "I was wrong. I'm good at climbing and jumping and physical stuff, but I'm terrible at working with others. I'm not patient. I don't like admitting when I'm wrong."

"But you're learning," Zip interjected quietly.

"I'm learning," Sophie agreed. "Because of them." She gestured at Morty and Zip. "They taught me fast isn't always best. That showing off isn't the same as being brave... and being remembered isn't as important as being a good friend."

Morty adjusted his spectacles and picked up the story. "I thought the quest needed planning. Organization. Someone smart to navigate and solve puzzles. I thought my maps and preparations would save us." He looked down at his paws. "I was wrong too. Or not wrong, exactly, but incomplete. Yes, we needed planning. But we also needed courage to trust when we couldn't see the way. We needed flexibility when plans didn't work." He looked at his friends. "We needed each other."

"Is it my turn?" Zip asked nervously. They confirmed it was.

His light pulsed as he gathered courage. "I didn't think they needed me at all. I thought I was too small, too scared, too dim to matter. I came along because I loved the tree, but I didn't think I'd actually help." His light brightened slightly. "But I did help. I found clues the others missed. I kept them from killing each other when they fought. I reminded them of what mattered when they forgot. My light might be small, but a small light is enough when it's in the right place at the right time."

Thornback listened without interrupting, his ancient eyes moving from one to the next. Something in his expression shifted. Softened, maybe. Or warmed.

"We fought," Sophie continued. "We said terrible things. I called Morty a coward."

"I called her selfish," Morty added quietly.

"We hurt Zip so badly he left," Sophie said, her voice breaking. "We were so focused on being right we didn't see we were destroying our friendship."

"But we found each other again," Zip said. "We apologized. We meant it. We built something better than what we had before."

"We learned," Sophie said. "That's the point, isn't it? We weren't perfect. We messed up. But we're trying to be better."

Silence fell over the grove. Thornback stared at them with those ancient, knowing eyes, the last rays of sunset painting everything gold and orange and making the starberries glow even brighter.

Finally ... finally ... the massive bear spoke.

"Forty winters ago, I was born beneath the Starberry Tree. My mother brought me there when I was just a cub, drawn by the light and the whispers. The tree welcomed us. Sheltered us. Showed us magic." He looked at the starberry bushes with something like love. "When I grew, I came here. Found this grove. Decided to guard it. Because magic is precious. Magic is rare. And magic should only go to those who understand its true nature."

"And what is its true nature?" Morty asked carefully.

"Magic isn't power," Thornback said. "Magic is connection. It's the light which brings creatures together. The whispers that guide them home. The tree which makes everyone feel like they belong." He looked at each of them in turn. "You understand that now. You didn't when you started ... you came seeking glory, seeking to prove yourselves, seeking to be special. But you learned. You failed. You hurt each other. And you chose to be better."

He paused, the air heavy with something unspoken.

"The tree is one," Thornback said slowly, his ancient eyes distant with memory. "But the magic is seven. Seven groves. Seven gifts. Seven chances to prove yourselves worthy. You've found the first. The others wait in places even I have not seen ... places to test you in ways this grove never could."

His voice grew quieter, more serious. "The ancient ones built something vast. Something that waits for those brave enough to seek it. You three have only just begun."

The weight of those words settled over them like a blanket. Seven groves. They'd thought finding one would be enough. But this was just the beginning.

Thornback stood and moved aside, no longer blocking the starberry bushes.

"Take three berries," he said. "Three for three travelers. Three for three lessons learned. Three to plant and restore the light."

They stared at him, then at the bushes, then back at him.

"You... you really mean it?" Sophie whispered.

"You are worthy," Thornback confirmed. "Not because you're perfect, but because you understand worthiness isn't about being perfect. It's about trying. Learning. Choosing friendship over pride."

They approached the bushes slowly, reverently. The berries glowed brighter as they got close, and the whispers grew louder ... still not quite words, but definitely welcoming. Definitely approving.

Yes, the whispers seemed to say. *Yes, little ones. Take what you need. Carry it home. Restore the light.*

Morty picked the first berry ... silver-white, glowing like moonlight. It was warm in his paws and hummed with magic making his fur stand on end.

Sophie picked the second ... golden-bright, radiant like sunshine. It pulsed with energy, making her tail fluff up involuntarily.

Zip picked the third ... soft blue-green, glowing like twilight. It was almost as big as his entire body but felt light and perfect when he held it, like it had been waiting specifically for him.

"Thank you," they said to Thornback, their voices full of wonder.

"Thank the tree," Thornback replied. "Thank the ancient ones who planted these groves. Thank the magic that chose you." He paused. "And thank each other. You saved yourselves before you saved the tree."

They carefully wrapped the starberries in soft leaves from Morty's satchel. The berries kept glowing even through the wrapping, casting soft light in three different colors.

"The journey home will be harder," Thornback warned. "It always is. You'll be tired. Tested. The forest will challenge you in ways you don't expect."

"We'll be ready," Sophie said.

"Agreed" Morty and Zip added.

Thornback nodded slowly. "I believe you will be."

As they turned to leave the grove, the whispers rose one more time ... louder, clearer, almost like actual words:

Go well, little heroes. Go safe. Go together. The light awaits.

They left the Deep Forest as the last light faded from the sky. Three starberries glowing in Morty's satchel like captured stars. Three friends walking side by side. Three heroes who'd found something more valuable than any magic.

But in the darkness behind them, in the deep places of the forest where the old magic still whispered and waited, something else was stirring. That presence that had been watching them since they left the archives. Something that knew about the ancient ones and the seven groves and the magic they'd only just begun to understand.

The shadows moved where shadows shouldn't move. And somewhere in the night, stone ground against stone.

The journey home was waiting... but so was something else.

CHAPTER EIGHT
Lost in the Mist

They left the Deep Forest as the last light faded from the sky, eager to put distance between themselves and whatever had been watching from the shadows. That feeling from back at the archives ... the stone grinding against stone, the sense of something ancient stirring ... had followed them to the grove. And even though Thornback had let them pass, even though they carried three glowing starberries wrapped in soft leaves, none of them felt safe.

"We should keep moving," Morty said, adjusting his satchel where the starberries pulsed with soft light. "Make camp somewhere closer to home."

Sophie agreed from the branches above. "The sooner we're out of the Deep Forest, the better."

Zip flew between them, his light steadier now after the grove, but flickering nervously. "Does anyone else feel like we're being followed?"

They all stopped and listened. The forest was settling into evening sounds ... birds finding roosts, small creatures heading to burrows. Normal sounds. Safe sounds.

Except for that feeling. The weight of eyes watching from the dark places between trees.

"Probably just nerves," Sophie said, though her tail twitched with unease.

"Probably," Morty agreed, though his paw went to his spectacles.

They kept walking as twilight deepened into dusk. The path was clear, Morty's map was accurate, and if they maintained good pace, they'd be home by tomorrow afternoon. They'd cross back over the Swift River in the morning, navigate through the Thornwood Thicket, and return to Thistlewood Forest as heroes. They'd save the tree. Everything would be fine.

Then the fog rolled in.

Not gradually. Not the way normal fog creeps through trees with evening air. This fog came fast ... thick and gray and cold, swallowing the forest in seconds like something hungry. Like something waiting.

The temperature dropped so suddenly Morty's breath formed clouds that disappeared into the larger cloud around them. The fog felt wrong against their fur ... too wet, almost oily, clinging to them like it was trying to seep inside.

And from somewhere in the gray thickness came a sound ... or what might have been a sound. Low and mournful, like wind through a cave, like an animal in pain, like nothing any of them had ever heard before. Or maybe it was just the fog itself, moving strangely through the trees.

It felt like the same sound they'd been hearing since the archives. The stone grinding. The presence following them through their entire quest.

And now it felt **here**.

"Stay together!" Sophie shouted, but the fog muffled her voice, made it sound distant and wrong. "Don't move! Just stay ... "

The sound came again, closer this time. And something seemed to move through the fog ... or the fog itself shifted in heavy, rhythmic patterns sounding like footsteps. Like stone scraping against stone. Getting closer. Or seeming to get closer.

Sophie's instincts screamed RUN and her legs obeyed before her brain could stop them. She bolted through the fog, branches whipping past her face, her heart hammering.

Zip's wings carried him straight up, away from the sound ... or away from where he thought the sound was coming from ... higher and higher into the gray thickness until he was completely surrounded by fog with no sense of which direction was down.

Morty froze, his paws going to his spectacles even though adjusting them couldn't make the fog any less thick or whatever might be in it any less terrifying.

And then, they were separated.

Something ... or the fog itself, or their own panic ... had driven them apart.

Sophie ran until her lungs burned and her legs ached, then forced herself to stop. Running without thinking is how you get lost. Running without thinking is how you get caught.

She stood panting in the fog, trying to hear anything over her own thundering heartbeat. The gray pressed in from all sides, thick enough she couldn't see her own paw held at arm's length.

Think. What would Morty do?

He'd orient himself. Find landmarks. Use logic instead of panic.

Sophie closed her eyes ... not that closing them made any difference in this thickness ... and forced herself to breathe slowly. In the climbing challenge, rushing had almost killed her. Morty's patience had saved her life.

She opened her eyes and looked around carefully. The fog was thick, but not completely uniform. There ... a slightly lighter patch where the fading sunlight was trying to break through. That was west. Which meant north was... She turned carefully, keeping her tail still so she could sense the air currents, using her whiskers to feel the space around her.

Something seemed to move in the fog ahead. Or the fog itself was shifting in strange ways.

Sophie froze, every muscle tense. A shape ... or what looked like a shape. Large. Too large. Moving in ways which made her skin crawl, though she couldn't say exactly why. Her mind kept trying to make sense of it ... limbs? branches? fog taking form? ... but nothing fit right.

The shape seemed to turn toward her. Or maybe she just imagined it did.

Sophie didn't run this time. She climbed. Straight up the nearest tree, her claws digging into bark, moving with the careful precision Morty had taught her. Test each handhold. Plan ahead. Don't rush.

From her perch high in the branches, she heard something below. Or thought she heard something. Breathing? Wind moving through the fog? She couldn't tell. A smell drifted up ... old earth and dampness and something made her fur stand on end. But was something hunting her? Or was she just so scared every sound felt like a threat?

Did something want the starberries? Or was that just what made sense to her terrified mind?

Then, faint through the fog, she heard Morty's voice calling her name.

Morty stood frozen for only a moment before his brain kicked into gear. Freezing was what prey did. He wasn't prey. He was a navigator, a planner, someone who solved problems.

The problem was: his friends were lost in fog with something ... or with nothing but their own fear ... and all his tools were useless. His map couldn't show him where they'd scattered. His compass couldn't point to Sophie or Zip.

But he had other senses. Underground senses. He could feel the shape of the land beneath his paws, sense the direction water ran, know which way led uphill or down. The fog might blind his eyes, but it couldn't blind the instincts bred into every mole.

He closed his eyes and trusted himself.

Then he heard Sophie's voice in the distance, faint and scared, calling for them.

Morty called back, describing the large oak tree next to him, the boulder looked vaguely turtle-shaped. His voice echoed strangely through the fog, but he kept talking, kept giving her landmarks to follow.

Something seemed to move past him in the fog ... or the fog itself shifted ... close enough he felt what might have been displacement of air, smelled something like old earth and stone. But was something there? Or was his terrified mind creating threats out of dampness and darkness?

He felt certain ... absolutely certain ... whatever it was had moved toward where Sophie's voice had come from.

"SOPHIE, CLIMB!" he shouted. "CLIMB NOW!"

A moment of terrible silence. Then Sophie's voice: "I'm up! I'm safe! Keep talking, I'll find you!"

Morty kept describing the tree, the boulder, the way the ground sloped slightly downward to his left. And slowly ... so slowly ... Sophie appeared through the gray, moving carefully from tree to tree, jumping when necessary but testing each landing.

They hugged without thinking about it, both breathing hard.

"Did you see it?" Sophie whispered.

"I... I don't know what I saw. Or felt. Or if there was anything there at all."

"I saw something. Or I think I did. But now I'm not sure if I really saw anything or just... scared myself."

They looked at each other, the same terrible thought forming: "Where's Zip?"

Zip was lost in the worst way possible.

He'd flown up to escape something ... or to escape his own terror ... but now he had no idea which direction was down. The fog surrounded him completely ... above, below, all around. Everything looked exactly the same. Thick. Gray. Cold.

His wings were exhausted from flying carefully, from trying not to make noise, from the constant effort of staying aloft in air that felt heavy and wet.

He was going to fall. Or get caught by something. Or both. Or maybe nothing would happen at all except he'd be lost forever.

Stop. Focus on the next step.

That's what he'd learned in the maze. He couldn't see everything, so he'd focus on what he could see. Which right now was... nothing. Just fog and fear.

Zip descended slowly, carefully, until his antennae touched something solid. A branch. He landed gratefully, his wings trembling with exhaustion.

Below him, something seemed to move through the fog. Or the fog was moving in rhythmic patterns. Like footsteps. Like the sounds that had scattered them. Like something circling his tree.

Or like wind moving through branches in regular intervals. Or like his imagination giving shape to formless mist.

Zip's light dimmed instinctively ... going small, going dark, trying to hide.

In the maze, going dark had meant getting lost forever. His light ... small as it was ... had been enough to guide him through. It had been enough to hold back the darkness.

Zip thought about Sophie and Morty out there somewhere, trying to find him. They couldn't see in this fog. But they could see light.

He thought about what Thornback had said: *Magic is connection. The light that brings creatures together.*

Zip stopped trying to hide his light. Instead, he made it brighter.

It was hard ... his whole life he'd gotten used to his light being weak, accepting it, never really pushing it to see what it could do. But now the point wasn't showing off or being impressive. The point was being a beacon for his friends.

The point was, sometimes being found is braver than hiding.

His light grew. Not as bright as his siblings, not spectacular. But bright enough to push back the fog around him. Bright enough to create a small sphere of warm golden glow.

Below him, something hissed ... or the wind shifted through the trees in a way sounding eerily like hissing. A horrible sound, like metal scraping on bone. Or like branches rubbing in just the wrong way.

And then whatever presence he'd felt seemed to pull back. Or maybe his light just made the fog retreat naturally. Or maybe there had never been anything there at all, and the relief he felt was just because he could finally see something besides gray.

"I'm here!" Zip shouted into the fog, his voice stronger now. "Sophie! Morty! Follow my light!"

And he kept it blazing, steady and sure. A small star in the mist.

They saw his light from thirty yards away ... a warm glow in all the cold gray.

"Zip!" they shouted.

Behind them, they heard something ... or thought they heard something. A sound like heavy footsteps crashing through undergrowth. Or maybe just branches breaking in the wind. Fast. Getting closer.

"Go!" Morty gasped. "Something's ... "

They ran toward Zip's light, Sophie in the lead, Morty scrambling behind. Something felt close ... they could hear sounds, it might be breathing, a smell like old earth and stone, vibrations that might be footfalls.

Or maybe it was just their own terror, their exhausted minds turning every sound into a threat. But it seemed so real.

Sophie hit the tree first and climbed faster than she'd ever climbed anything. Morty was right behind her ... moles can climb when properly motivated by fear ... his claws scrabbling on bark, his satchel bouncing wildly.

They reached Zip's branch just as something ... or nothing ... seemed to arrive below them.

In the sphere of Zip's golden light, they thought they saw something. Or almost saw something. Or maybe the fog was just playing tricks.

Large. Too large. The fog seemed to shift and take shape ... sometimes looking like stone come alive, sometimes like shadow given form, sometimes like nothing but mist and fear and exhaustion. Were those eyes glowing dull red? Or just Zip's light reflecting strangely off the fog? The shape ... if there was a shape ... kept changing, refusing to hold still long enough to know if it was real.

Did something want the starberries? Or were they just so scared and tired every shadow seemed hungry for what they carried?

And if something was real... what would it do to get them?

Something seemed to reach upward ... limbs or branches or fog tendrils, impossible to tell ... stretching toward the tree.

Zip's light blazed brighter. The warm glow intensified, pushing down through the fog.

Below them, something shrieked. The scary metal-on-bone sound they'd heard before. ...or maybe it was just wind through the trees.... or branches scraping,.... or ?? ...

Whatever it was ... or wasn't ... seemed to fall back.

"Your light ... " Sophie started, then stopped. Was his light holding something back? Or just pushing away fog? Or giving them courage in the face of nothing at all?

But Zip was shaking with effort, his small body trembling. "I can't... keep this up much longer..."

Morty fumbled with his satchel and pulled out his lantern. It was weak compared to Zip's glow, but it added more light to the sphere around them.

Below, something hissed ... or the wind shifted ... and whatever presence they'd felt seemed to retreat. Not running. Not scared. Just... pulling back. The sensation of being watched grew distant. Then more distant still.

Or maybe they'd just stopped being quite so terrified, and the fog was just fog again.

For a long moment, they held their breath, waiting.

Then, slowly, the fog began to lift. Not naturally ... not the way morning sun burns fog away. This fog retreated quickly. Pulled back. Like something had called it away.

By the time they climbed down from the tree, they could see clearly again. The evening stars were visible through the canopy. The forest looked completely normal. Nothing lurked in the shadows. No creature waited below.

Had there ever been one? Or had they just panicked in the fog, their fear creating monsters out of mist?

"Did you see it?" Sophie asked quietly. "Really see it?"

"I... I don't know," Morty admitted. "I thought I did. But now..." He looked around at the normal, peaceful forest. "Maybe we just scared ourselves?"

"My light pushed something back," Zip said, but his voice was uncertain. "I felt it. But... what if it was just the fog? What if there was nothing there at all?"

They stood in uncomfortable silence, not sure what they'd experienced. Not sure what was real.

"The starberries," Morty whispered, checking his satchel with shaking paws.

They were still there, still glowing. But dimmer now. Not much ... just slightly less bright than before.

"They're fading," Morty said. "How long do we have?" questioned Sophie.

Morty studied the berries carefully, his mind calculating. "I don't know. A day? Maybe two? But the longer we take, the dimmer they get. And if they fade completely..."

He didn't need to finish. They all understood. If the starberries died before they reached home, this entire quest was for nothing.

"Then we need to move," Sophie said firmly. "Now. Fast. Whether that thing was real or not, we need to get home."

"The Swift River is this way," Morty pointing north. "But I'm not sure... with the fog, we might have gotten turned around. My map is ... " He stopped and looked at it, and his face fell. The fog had soaked through everything. The map was there, but the ink had run, the details smudged and unclear.

For a moment, none of them spoke.

Then Zip said quietly, "We don't need the map. We know the way. The river is north. The thicket is beyond that. Home is past the thicket."

"But without the map ... " Morty started.

"We have each other," Sophie interrupted. "You know which way is north even without a compass. I can navigate the terrain from the trees. Zip can see from above. We don't need a map. We need to trust ourselves."

Morty looked at his ruined map, then at his friends, then at the glowing starberries... slowly, steadily dimming.

He folded the map carefully and tucked it away..

They set off north through the darkening forest, moving as quickly as they dared. Behind them, in the deep shadows between ancient trees... something watched them go.

Or maybe nothing watched at all... or maybe their fear itself had eyes.

The starberries pulsed with fading light. Time was running out. And home had never felt so far away.

Twisted alternate paths in the deep forest and fog.

CHAPTER NINE

The Storm

They'd been walking for about an hour when the sky changed.

Clouds gathered on the horizon, the air grew heavy, and that electric smell hit them ... the one which says rain is coming whether you're ready or not. Morty's underground instincts prickled. Bad weather ahead. They needed to move faster.

Sophie was already picking up her pace. "How far to the river?"

Morty pulled out his map with shaking paws. The fog had soaked through everything ... the ink was smudged, details blurred and unclear. He squinted at what remained. "Maybe two miles? Hard to tell now. The map is damaged."

Zip flew closer, his voice tight with nervousness. "Can you read it at all?"

"Some of it. Enough, I think." Morty's voice didn't sound as confident as his words. Without the map's details, they'd have to rely on memory and instinct. "We need to hurry."

The wind picked up, making trees bend and creak. Leaves swirled through the air. The clouds looked angry now, dark and heavy and moving fast. Behind them, something felt wrong. That same presence from the fog. Or maybe just the storm's approach making everything feel ominous.

Then the rain hit.

Not gradually ... all at once, like the sky had been holding its breath and finally let go. Hard, angry drops that soaked through fur instantly, turned the ground to mud, made it impossible to see more than a few feet ahead.

Sophie shouted over the roar of water hitting leaves. "I can't see!"

Morty called back, his voice barely audible through the deluge. "Follow my voice! The river should be just ahead!"

Zip struggled most of all. Each raindrop hit him like a boulder, threatening to knock him from the sky. His wings were getting heavier, waterlogged, barely keeping him aloft. Sophie shouted for him to land on her head, and he didn't argue. He dropped into her fur, tucking himself down, trying to keep his wings dry. His light dimmed to almost nothing.

They burst through a line of trees and stopped.

The Swift River wasn't swift anymore ... it was furious. Brown water churned and foamed, carrying broken branches downstream at terrifying speeds. The log they'd crossed days ago was gone, either swept away or submerged. The sound alone was overwhelming ... a deep roar like the river itself was angry.

Morty had to shout to be heard. "We can't cross here!"

Sophie pointed back at the forest behind them, where water was already pooling, the forest floor beginning to flood. "We can't stay either! The whole area's going underwater!"

She was right. The water was rising fast, already ankle-deep and climbing.

"Upstream!" Morty took off at a run. "Higher ground!"

They followed the riverbank upstream, fighting wind and rain and rising water. Morty's paws kept slipping in mud. Sophie's fur was so waterlogged she felt three times her normal weight. Zip just held on, feeling utterly helpless. The water reached Morty's chest when they found it ... an ancient stone wall stretching across the river, about two feet wide at the top.

Water crashed against it, sending spray high into the air, but the wall held firm.

Sophie pointed, her voice cutting through the storm. "That! We can cross on that!"

Morty stared at the wall, then at the churning water on either side. "That's insane!"

"Do you have a better idea?"

A wave crashed against the wall, sending spray twenty feet up. They looked at each other through the rain, water still rising around them. There was no other option.

Sophie's voice steadied now that they'd decided. "Morty goes first. Test the footing. I'll go last."

Morty wanted to argue. Everything in him wanted to argue. But she was right. He muttered something about really hating this while adjusting his spectacles, even though it was pointless with all the water.

He stepped onto the wall.

The surface was slippery ... moss and rain and centuries of weather making it treacherous. The wind pushed at him immediately. The spray made it hard to see. And the sound ... the constant roar ... made it impossible to think. Sophie called encouragement from behind, telling him slow and steady.

Morty took another step, testing his weight, using his tunnel-navigation sense of balance.

Halfway across, his paw slipped. For one horrible moment, he teetered toward the raging water, his arms windmilling, his mind going completely blank with terror. Then his underground instincts kicked in ... the same instincts which guided him through dark tunnels. His paws scrambled, found purchase, caught the edge. He pulled himself back onto the wall, gasping.

His voice shook when he called back. "I'm okay! Keep coming!"

He made it to the far side and collapsed on the bank, his whole body trembling. From across the raging water, he shouted for Sophie to come, his voice hoarse with fear and relief.

Sophie took a deep breath and spoke quietly to Zip, still tucked in her fur. "Hold tight."

Zip's tiny voice was muffled but certain. "I'm holding. I believe in you."

Those words made Sophie stand taller. Someone was trusting her. She couldn't let him down. She stepped onto the wall, immediately feeling how slippery the stone was. Her magnificent tail ... currently soaked and bedraggled ... spread out for balance. Morty called encouragement from the other side, his voice cutting through the storm's roar.

Step by careful step. The wind pushed at her sideways. The spray made it impossible to see clearly. And the weight of Zip, tiny as he was, reminded her with every movement that one wrong step would doom them both.

Three-quarters across, a massive wave hit the wall. Not spray. A full wave, reaching up like the river had a watery hand and wanted to knock them off. Sophie felt her paws lose contact with the stone, felt herself being swept sideways, felt Zip's tiny legs gripping her fur with desperate strength. She was falling ...

Her claws caught a crack in the stone. A tiny imperfection that her squirrel reflexes found automatically.

She held on.

The wave drained away. Sophie hung from the side of the wall by just her claws, Zip still clutching her head, both suspended over the raging water. Morty's scream cut through even the storm's roar. Every muscle burned. Her claws felt like they were being torn out. But she pulled ... pulled with every ounce of squirrel strength, pulled with desperation, pulled because a tiny firefly was counting on her. Her paw found the top of the wall. Then another. She scrambled back up, gasping, water streaming from her fur.

"Still okay, Zip?" Her voice came out as barely a whisper.

His tiny response was equally quiet. "Still okay. Still holding on."

The last quarter of the crossing felt like it took forever. Every muscle screamed. Every nerve was on fire. But she kept going until finally ... finally ... her paws touched solid ground on the far bank. She collapsed next to Morty while Zip crawled out of her fur, wings bedraggled but safe.

For a long moment, none of them could speak.

Zip finally broke the silence, his whisper barely audible. "We did it."

Morty managed a slight smile despite his trembling. "We almost died."

"But we didn't." Sophie's voice was firm despite her exhaustion.

Through the rain, barely visible, Sophie spotted a rocky outcropping with an overhang. She pointed, too tired for more words than necessary. "There. Shelter."

They stumbled toward it and found a shallow cave. Not deep, but enough. The ground inside was dry. They collapsed just inside the entrance, all three of them shaking ... from cold, from exhaustion, from the adrenaline of almost dying twice in ten minutes.

Morty pulled supplies from his waterproof satchel with trembling paws. Within minutes, he had a small fire going. The warmth was incredible, almost painful against their frozen skin. They huddled close to the flames, wrapped in slightly damp blankets, not speaking. Just breathing. Just being alive.

Sophie's paws wouldn't stop shaking. Morty kept adjusting his spectacles even though they didn't need adjusting. Zip's light flickered erratically, unable to find a steady rhythm. The rain continued outside, a constant drumming making the cave feel even smaller, even more isolated from the world.

After what felt like an eternity, Morty's breathing finally slowed to something close to normal. His paws steadied enough to reach for his satchel. "I should check the starberries. Make sure they survived the crossing."

He opened the satchel with careful paws and pulled out the leaf-wrapped bundle. Then he froze, his entire body going rigid.

Sophie's voice was careful, controlled. "Morty? What's wrong?"

Morty's paw trembled as he unwrapped the leaves. The firelight caught the starberries and his breath stopped completely. They were dying. Not dimmer. Not fading. *Dying.* The glow had been steady and bright in the grove now flickered like candles in wind. The golden berry pulsed weakly

... on, off, on, off ... like a heartbeat struggling to continue. The silver one had darkened to dull gray, with only occasional sparks of light. The blue-green berry was the worst: it barely glowed at all, just the faintest flicker deep inside, like an ember about to go out.

"No." The word escaped Morty as barely more than a breath. "No, no, no."

Sophie crawled over immediately, her exhaustion forgotten. When she saw the berries, her tail went completely still, all animation draining from her body. "How long do we have?"

Morty's mind raced, calculating, comparing their current state to how they'd looked at the grove, in the fog, this morning. His scientific brain catalogued every detail: the rate of dimming, the irregular pulsing, the way the light seemed to be withdrawing inward. When he finally spoke, his voice cracked with the weight of the answer. "Hours. Maybe less." He looked up at his friends, eyes wet with unshed tears. "We almost died out there for nothing."

Sophie's voice turned fierce, cutting through his despair. "Not for nothing. We're alive. We're here. We still have time."

"Do we?" Morty held up the berries, watching them flicker pathetically in his paws. "Look at them, Sophie. They're dying faster than we can move."

Zip flew closer, his own dim light reflecting off the fading starberries. "Can we do anything? To help them?"

Morty's voice rose with panic, all his careful control shattering. "I don't know! I don't know what they need! Warmth? Light? Magic?" He stood up, pacing frantically, his words tumbling over each other. "All my planning, all my preparation, and I never thought ... I never considered ... "

Sophie's paw caught his shoulder, stopping him mid-pace. "Stop. You're spiraling. We need to think."

"Think about what? We can't fix this!"

"We can try." Sophie took the golden berry from Morty's trembling paws, studying it with intense focus. The warmth that pulsed against her chest during the journey felt fainter now, weaker. But it was still there, still fighting. "They're not dead yet. Which means there's still hope."

Morty took a shaking breath, adjusted his spectacles, forced his scientist brain back online. His training, his natural tendency toward analysis ... it all kicked in, overriding the panic. "You're right. Okay. What do we know about starberries?"

Zip offered the obvious. "They glow."

Sophie added more. "They're magic."

"They came from the grove." Morty's mind started working faster, connections forming. "They were planted by the ancient ones. They need..." He trailed off, thinking hard. "What sustained them in the grove? What kept them alive for centuries?"

Sophie's voice was slow, thoughtful. "The tree. The original Starberry Tree. It's where the grove's magic came from."

Morty's hope deflated as quickly as it had risen. "But we don't have the tree. We're trying to GET to the tree."

Zip's voice was quiet but certain, cutting through their despair with unexpected clarity. "We don't have the tree. But we have its magic. A little bit."

They both turned to look at him, seeing him hover there with his dim but steady light, understanding dawning on their faces.

Zip flew closer to the fading starberries, his words coming faster now. "The tree gave us these berries. Which means it gave us a piece of itself. A piece of its light. Maybe... maybe they just need to remember they're not alone?"

Morty adjusted his spectacles, his scientific mind wrestling with the concept. "That's not very scientific."

Sophie's response was immediate and practical. "The berries are literally magic. Maybe science isn't the answer."

Morty looked at the dying berries, then at his friends, then back at the berries. The scientist in him wanted to argue, to find a logical solution. But the part of him that had learned to trust, to believe in things beyond maps and calculations ... *that part* won. "Okay. What do we try?"

They experimented.

Morty carefully moved the berries closer to the fire, not too close ... he didn't want to burn them ... but close enough for warmth. The golden berry flickered slightly brighter for a moment, responding to the heat. Then it dimmed again, settling back to its weak pulse. Morty made mental notes, his voice analytical. "Warmth helps. But it's not enough."

Sophie unwrapped her driest blanket and created a nest of soft fabric, her paws moving with careful precision. "What if they need to be comfortable? Protected?" She gently placed all three berries in the nest, wrapped them carefully like precious eggs. The silver berry pulsed once, twice, then settled back to its irregular flicker. Sophie watched it intently. "Better. But still not enough."

Zip hovered over the nest, his light shining down on the berries with focused intensity. "What if they need light? Not just warmth, but actual light?" He concentrated, pushing his glow as bright as he could manage. His whole body strained with effort, trembling in the air.

For a moment ... just a moment ... the blue-green berry responded. Its glow strengthened noticeably, synchronized with Zip's light, pulsed in perfect harmony like two hearts beating as one. Then Zip's exhaustion caught up with him. His light flickered and dimmed, his wings faltering. The blue-green berry faded back to almost nothing.

Sophie's voice filled with excitement. "It worked! Zip, it worked! They responded to your light!"

Zip was breathing hard, his wings trembling as he struggled to stay airborne. "I can't... I can't keep it up. I'm too tired. Too dim."

Morty's mind was already racing with new calculations, new possibilities. "You don't have to keep it up forever. Just... maybe periodically? Like feeding them? A burst of light every hour to keep them going?"

Zip nodded weakly, landing on a nearby rock to rest. "I can try."

They settled into a rhythm. Zip would rest, gathering his strength, conserving energy. Then he'd fly over and shine as brightly as he could for thirty seconds, maybe a minute ... as long as his exhausted body could manage. The starberries would respond each time, not dramatically, but noticeably. Their glow would strengthen slightly, stabilize, hold for a while before slowly dimming again.

It wasn't a solution. But it bought them time.

Sophie kept her paw on the nest between Zip's light-feedings, her body heat adding constant warmth. Morty tended the fire with scientific precision, keeping it at optimal temperature, checking the berries constantly, tracking their condition with careful observation.

They were so focused on the starberries they almost didn't hear it.

A sound from outside the cave. Low. Deep. Like stone grinding against stone.

All three of them froze, their bodies going rigid with recognition and dread.

Sophie's whisper was barely audible. "Please tell me that's just the storm."

The sound came again. Closer now. Not grinding ... breathing. Heavy, slow breathing echoing strangely in the rain, resonating in a way that natural sounds shouldn't.

Zip's light flared instinctively, panic overriding exhaustion, his body reacting before his mind could catch up.

And outside the cave, something moved.

They couldn't see it clearly ... just a massive shadow in the rain, darker than the storm clouds, moving in ways which didn't quite make sense. Too big. Too strange. Sometimes it looked like it was walking on two legs, sometimes four, sometimes it seemed to flow like water or smoke, never quite settling into one form.

Morty's voice was tight with the fear they all felt. "It followed us. From the fog. From the forest. It's been following us the whole time."

The shadow circled the cave entrance slowly, deliberately. Testing. Searching for weaknesses or perhaps just making its presence known.

Sophie's claws extended instinctively, her body tensing for a fight she wasn't sure she could win. "What does it want?"

Morty's analytical mind cut through the fear with cold logic. "The starberries. It has to be the starberries. Ancient magic attracts... whatever that is."

The breathing sound intensified, becoming louder, more present. The shadow moved closer to the entrance, its form shifting and flowing in the rain-soaked darkness.

Zip flew to position himself between the entrance and the nest of starberries, his tiny body shaking but his light blazing as bright as he could make it despite his exhaustion. The golden glow pushed back the darkness at the cave entrance just slightly, creating a barrier of illumination.

The shadow recoiled.

Not much. Just a little. Like it had touched something hot, something that caused actual pain or discomfort.

Sophie's voice was filled with wonder and hope. "Your light. Zip, it doesn't like your light."

Zip's voice was strained, tight with the effort of maintaining his glow. "I can't keep this up forever. I'm already exhausted from trying to help the berries."

Morty's practical mind was already working on solutions. "You don't have to. We take turns. We rest in shifts. One of us always awake, watching. If that thing tries to come in, Zip lights up and drives it back."

Sophie asked the question none of them wanted to answer. *"And if that doesn't work?"*

No one responded. The silence was answer enough.

The shadow circled one more time, its movements deliberate and patient. Then it settled into a position just outside the cave, visible as a darker patch against the storm. Not leaving. Not attacking. Just... waiting.

They could hear its breathing. Steady. Patient. Like it had all the time in the world and was content to use it.

Sophie's voice was quiet but practical. "We can't stay here forever. The starberries won't last. And that thing isn't leaving."

Morty tried to sound more confident than he felt. "Then we rest now. Get what sleep we can. At first light, we move. Fast as we possibly can."

Zip added what they were all thinking. "And hope that thing doesn't follow."

Morty's grim response killed the hope. "It'll follow. But maybe in daylight, with the tree close, we'll have a chance."

They organized shifts quickly and efficiently. Sophie would take first watch ... she was used to being alert at night, used to scanning for predators from her treetop home. Morty would take second ... his underground senses worked better in darkness anyway, evolved for life beneath the earth. Zip would take third, keeping his light ready in case the shadow tried anything.

Sophie positioned herself at the cave entrance, her back to the fire's warmth, eyes fixed on the shadow outside. It was still there, still breathing, still waiting with infinite patience. She kept one paw on the nest of starberries, feeling them pulse weakly against her fur, their rhythm irregular and concerning.

Her whisper was so quiet even Morty and Zip couldn't hear, meant only for the dying lights in her paws. "Don't give up. We're almost there. We're almost home. Just hold on a little longer. Please."

The golden berry pulsed once under her paw. Just once. Like it heard her. Like it was trying to answer, to promise it would keep fighting.

Behind her, Morty and Zip huddled near the fire, wrapped in blankets that were finally starting to dry. They didn't sleep ... not really ... just dozed fitfully, jerking awake at every sound, every shift in the fire, every change in the breathing outside.

The hours crawled by with agonizing slowness.

During Morty's watch, he sat with his ruined map spread across his knees, studying it by firelight even though he'd memorized every remaining detail. His broken spectacles made everything blur into vague shapes and shadows, but he traced the route home anyway, his claw following the path they'd need to take. The Swift River ... they'd crossed it, survived it. The Thornwood Thicket ... still ahead, still waiting. Then home. Maybe five miles total. Five miles feeling like fifty, like a hundred, like an impossible distance.

He whispered to himself, the words a mantra against fear. "I can do this blind if I have to. Underground navigation. Trust your instincts. You've got this."

The shadow outside shifted slightly, a barely perceptible movement that still made Morty's paw instinctively reach for his satchel, ready to wake Zip if needed. But the shadow settled again, still just watching, still waiting with terrible patience.

Morty checked the starberries, his scientific mind automatically cataloguing their condition. Still flickering. Still dying, but slower now with Zip's periodic light-feedings buying them precious time. He did the math in his head: current rate of decline, distance remaining, average travel speed accounting for exhaustion and obstacles. The numbers were close. Too close. They'd need everything to go perfectly. No delays. No obstacles. No ...

The shadow moved again, and Morty stopped thinking about the future. Right now, staying alive until dawn was enough.

During Zip's watch, he positioned himself at the cave entrance, his small light creating a sphere of warm golden glow that pushed back the darkness just slightly, just enough to see a few feet into the storm.

The shadow was still there. He could see it more clearly now than Sophie or Morty had ... could see how it seemed to shift and change, never quite holding one shape for more than a few seconds. Sometimes it looked almost animal, with suggestions of limbs and eyes. Sometimes almost plant-like, with reaching branches or roots. Sometimes like nothing from the natural world at all, just darkness given form and purpose.

His light flickered with fear, and the shadow responded immediately, moving closer as if sensing weakness.

Zip forced his glow to steady, drawing on reserves he didn't know he had. The words came as a whisper, a reminder to himself. "I'm enough. I don't have to be the brightest. I just have to be a light."

His glow strengthened despite his exhaustion. Not much ... he was too tired for much ... but enough. The shadow pulled back slightly, maintaining its distance, respecting the boundary of illumination.

They stayed like that for an hour: Zip glowing steadily at the entrance, the shadow waiting in the rain, both of them patient in their own way. Both of them determined. One to protect, one to... what? They still didn't know what it wanted, not really.

When the first hint of dawn began to gray the sky, turning the world from black to charcoal, Zip flew back to his friends and touched Morty's shoulder gently with one wing.

His voice was quiet but urgent. **“It’s time.”**

CHAPTER TEN

Almost Home

Sophie woke to the smell of smoke.

Her eyes snapped open. The fire had burned down to embers, casting barely any light. The cave was cold. And outside ...

Dawn. The sky was the pale gray that comes just before sunrise, when the world is caught between night and day.

She sat up carefully, every muscle protesting. Beside her, Morty was already awake, his spectacles catching the faint light as he stared at his satchel.

"The starberries," he whispered.

Sophie's stomach dropped. "How bad?"

Morty opened the satchel with trembling paws. The three starberries lay wrapped in their leaves, still glowing. But the light was so dim now, so weak, like candles about to go out.

"We have hours," Morty said, his voice tight. "Maybe less. We need to move. Now."

Zip woke at the sound of their voices, his own light flickering to life. When he saw the berries, he went very still. "Will they last?"

"If we hurry." Morty was already packing, his paws moving with efficient urgency. "No delays. No stops. Straight home."

They left the cave within minutes, the sunrise painting the sky in shades of pink and gold. It should have been beautiful. Instead, it just reminded them that time was passing. Every second the sun rose higher was a second the starberries grew dimmer.

They moved fast ... faster than they'd moved the entire quest. Sophie led from the ground for once, her legs eating up distance despite the exhaustion weighing down every limb. Morty kept pace beside her, his shorter legs working double-time. Zip flew above, guiding them around obstacles, his light a steady beacon even though his wings trembled with fatigue.

The forest felt different in the early morning. Familiar. The trees were ones they recognized, the paths ones they'd walked before. They were getting close to home.

"Do you smell it?" Sophie asked suddenly, slowing.

Morty's nose twitched. "Smoke. And... something else."

They rounded a bend and stopped.

The Thornwood Thicket had grown back.

Not just grown back ... exploded. Where there had been a narrow path through the thorny bushes just days ago, now there was a solid wall of twisted branches and razor-sharp thorns, stretching as far as they could see in either direction.

"No," Sophie breathed. "No, no, no. We cleared this. We went through here."

"The magic," Morty said, his paw going to his spectacles. "The forest's magic is failing. It's trying to protect itself. Seal its boundaries."

"We don't have time to go around," Zip said, his voice rising with panic. "We don't have time to ... "

"Then we go through," Sophie interrupted. She looked at the wall of thorns, then at her friends, then at Morty's satchel where the starberries pulsed weakly. "We have everything we need. We've done harder things than this."

"Sophie ... " Morty started.

"Remember the cave challenges?" Sophie said, her mind already working. "We each had our own path. Our own skill to use. This is the same thing. One last test."

She pointed up. "Zip, you fly above and guide. Tell us where the thorns are thinnest, where the gaps are."

Then to Morty: "You navigate. Feel the ground. Find where the roots are weakest, where the earth gives way. Underground instincts."

"And you?" Morty asked.

"I climb. When we hit solid walls, I go up and over, find the route, call it down." Sophie's tail swished with determination. "Using everything we've learned. Everything we've become."

They looked at each other. No time for doubt. No time for fear.

"Together!," they all said at the same time.

The Thornwood Thicket was exactly as terrible as Sophie remembered, only worse.

The thorns grabbed at fur and skin like they were alive and angry. The branches twisted in impossible ways, forcing them to crawl, climb, squeeze through gaps barely large enough for Morty's satchel. But this time, they worked as a perfect unit.

"Left!" Zip called from above. "There's an opening three feet left!"

Morty's paws pressed against the earth. "The ground's softer here. The roots don't go deep. Push through!"

Sophie climbed a particularly dense section, her claws finding holds in the bark, her patient precision ... learned from Morty ... keeping her safe. From her vantage point, she could see the pattern. "There's a gap ahead! Straight through, then bear right!"

Her leg ... the one she'd injured in the climbing challenge ... throbbed with every movement. She felt it pull, felt the old wound protest even though the tree's magic had healed the scar. The muscle remembered the injury, and with each leap and climb it screamed at her to stop. But she didn't stop. Didn't slow. Just kept moving, kept leading, because someone had to.

They were halfway through when Morty suddenly stopped.

"What's wrong?" Sophie hissed.

Morty was staring at his spectacles. The left lens ... the one that had cracked during the swimming challenge ... had finally broken free completely. It lay in his paw, useless.

"I can barely see," he whispered.

Sophie's heart clenched. But then she remembered something. "Close your eyes."

"What?"

"Trust me. Close your eyes. Use your underground senses. Like in the fog. Like in the water. You don't need to see. You know the way."

Morty hesitated, then closed his eyes. His paws touched the ground. His whiskers twitched, reading the air. And slowly ... so slowly ... he nodded.

"I can feel it. The path. It's..." He opened his one good eye and smiled slightly. "This way."

He led them through the last section blind to sight but certain in sense, his paws guiding them around hidden thorns, through gaps they couldn't see, trusting instincts over vision.

When they finally burst out the other side, all three of them collapsed on the grass, breathing hard, bleeding from a dozen small cuts, exhausted beyond measure.

But they'd made it.

"How much time?" Sophie gasped.

Morty checked the starberries. His face went pale. "They're barely glowing. We have an hour. Maybe."

"How far to the tree?"

"Two miles."

"Then we run."

They ran.

Not the careful pace of a long journey. Not the measured speed of people conserving energy. They ran like their lives ... like their entire world ... depended on it.

Sophie's injured leg gave out first. Not completely, but enough so she stumbled, caught herself, felt the sharp spike of pain shoot up from ankle to hip. She gritted her teeth and kept running, but now there was a hitch in her stride, a limp she couldn't hide.

The memories came as she ran. Her parents packing their nest, preparing for a journey they'd never explained. Herself, small and confused, watching them work. "Where are you going?" she'd asked. "Somewhere better," her mother had said, not looking at her. "Can I come?" Silence. The worst silence. Then her father: "You're not ready yet. Stay here. Be good. Maybe we'll come back."

They never had.

Sophie had spent every day since trying to prove she was ready, was good enough, was worth coming back for. Every spectacular climb, every impossible jump, every risk had been trying to prove to parents who weren't watching that she mattered.

But running now ... lungs burning, leg screaming, starberries dying ... she realized something. She wasn't running toward glory or recognition or proof of her worth. She was running toward home. Not the nest where she'd been left behind, but the real home she'd found ... the clearing with the tree, the animals who'd accepted her, the friends who'd chosen to stay.

The young squirrel who wanted to learn climbing. The badger's granddaughter too scared to leave her burrow. Zip, who'd felt too dim to matter. Morty, who'd been too anxious to be brave. These were the animals she was running for. Not for applause, but because they needed her.

Worthiness wasn't about being spectacular or unbreakable. It was about showing up. About trying. About being willing to break and still keep going.

Her leg gave out again. This time she went down, hitting the ground hard, crying out as pain exploded through her injured limb.

Morty stopped immediately, turning back. "I'm okay," Sophie gasped, pushing herself up. "Just... give me a second."

"Your leg ... "

"I know. It doesn't matter. We keep going."

"Sophie ... "

"We keep going, Morty." Her voice was fierce despite the tears. "We're too close. I'm not stopping now."

Zip flew down, his light dim with exhaustion. "I can't carry you. I'm too small."

"I don't need carrying." Sophie forced herself to stand, testing the leg. "I just need to keep moving. One step at a time. We can do that, right?"

Morty adjusted his broken spectacles. "One step at a time."

They started again. Slower now ... Sophie limping badly, Morty stumbling over roots he couldn't see clearly, Zip's flight growing erratic as his wings faltered.

Morty checked the starberries again without stopping. The warmth was fading fast, the berries cooling like embers being snuffed out. The golden one flickered irregularly. The silver had darkened to almost nothing. The blue-green was so dim he could barely feel it anymore.

"Morty?" Sophie's voice was careful. "How bad?"

"Don't ask."

"That bad?"

"Just... keep moving."

Zip's wings finally gave out. He dropped onto Sophie's head, tucking into her fur, his tiny body trembling. "I'm sorry. I can't... I can't fly anymore."

"It's okay," Sophie said, even though the extra weight made her injured leg scream. "We're almost there. Just a little further."

The trees began to thin. Familiar trees now ... the split oak, the turtle boulder, the berry clearing. Home. They were almost home.

And then Sophie saw it.

Through the trees ahead, the clearing. The Starberry Tree.

Sophie's heart stopped. It looked worse than when they'd left. So much worse. The decay had spread further up the trunk. Branches hung even more limp, some already falling. The smell reached them even from here ... acrid and final.

"Are we too late?" Zip whispered.

Morty pulled out the starberries one last time. They were so dim now, barely glowing at all. "We're here. That's what matters. We made it."

The crowd had seen them now. Heads turning, voices rising. Sophie felt every eye turn toward them, felt the weight of all hope pressing down.

Her leg nearly gave out again. She caught herself, forced her body upright, refused to limp. Not now. Not when everyone was watching.

"Are you ready?" Morty whispered.

"No," Sophie admitted.

"Me neither," Zip added.

"Same," Morty finished.

They looked at each other and found strength in honesty. In friendship. In everything they'd become.

"Let's save a tree," Sophie said.

"Let's go home," Morty added.

"I'm all in," a soft whisper came from Zip.

And they stepped into the clearing

.

The Ancient Starberry Tree, dying... needs the magical starberries from our heros

CHAPTER ELEVEN
The Planting

The clearing was packed with animals. Hundreds of them ... maybe thousands. Rabbits and deer, foxes and badgers, birds filling every branch of every tree. They stood in absolute silence, their eyes fixed on the three small figures emerging from the forest.

Sophie's paws trembled as she stepped forward. Every face in the crowd was watching her. Waiting. Hoping. Depending on three animals who'd left as failures and had to return as heroes. Behind the crowd, the Starberry Tree rose dark and silent against the sky. Not just dark ... dying. The bark that had once shimmered with inner light was cracked and peeling now, branches hanging limp and brittle like bones left too long in the sun.

"It's worse," Zip whispered, his light flickering with horror. "So much worse than when we left."

Morty's paw clutched his satchel tighter. Inside, the starberries pulsed so faintly they were almost invisible. "We need to move. Now."

The crowd parted as they walked forward, creating a path to the tree. Sophie felt every eye on them, heard whispers threading through the silence ... some hopeful, some doubtful, some desperate. "They're so small," someone murmured. Another voice added, "They're just children." A third whispered the question that made Sophie's legs feel like water: "What if it doesn't work?"

The doubt echoed in her head like a drumbeat. What if they'd come all this way, survived everything, and it still wasn't enough? What if she froze in front of all these watching eyes, just like she'd frozen when her parents left?

Then a familiar voice cut through the whispers. "They made it." Ophelia's ancient eyes shone with tears as she flew down to meet them. "You actually made it."

"We brought the starberries," Morty said, his voice shaking. "Three of them. From the Deep Forest grove. But Ophelia, the tree ... "

"I know." The old owl's voice cracked. "It's been getting worse every day. The magic is nearly gone. The whispers stopped completely this morning."

She looked at the three of them ... really looked at them ... and something in her expression shifted. "You've changed."

"We had to," Sophie said quietly. "To survive."

"To succeed," Zip added.

"To become who we needed to be," Morty finished.

Ophelia nodded slowly, her ancient wisdom seeing something in them that perhaps they couldn't yet see in themselves. "Then you're ready. The tree is waiting."

She led them through the last of the crowd to the base of the Starberry Tree. Up close, it was even worse. The wrongness spreading from the roots pulsed with each passing moment, like a heartbeat running backwards, pulling life away instead of pushing it forward. The smell was all wrong too ... not the sweet scent of living wood but something acrid and final.

"Where do we plant them?" Sophie asked.

Ophelia gestured to three spots at the tree's base, equidistant from each other, forming a triangle around the trunk. "There. The old texts say the planting must form a circle of three. And it must be done by those who earned them." She paused, her gaze steady and serious. "All three of you."

Morty carefully pulled out the starberries with trembling paws. In the fading afternoon light, they glowed so weakly it was hard to tell if they still had any magic left at all. The golden berry's pulse was irregular and stuttering, the silver barely sparked, and the blue-green was the faintest ember, almost extinguished. He handed one to Sophie, one to Zip, and kept one for himself.

Sophie looked down at the berry in her paw. It was warm despite everything, still alive, humming with something she couldn't name but could feel ... like hope made solid, like light given form. But it was also dying, fading even as she held it, the warmth growing fainter with each passing second.

"What if I do it wrong?" The words escaped before she could stop them. "What if I'm not enough? What if ... "

"Then we fail together," Morty said quietly. "And we face whatever comes next.... **as a Team**."

"I'm terrified," Zip admitted.

"Me too," Sophie whispered.

"Same," Morty added.

They looked at each other ... three friends who'd left as strangers, three heroes who were still scared and imperfect but changed in ways that mattered. The crowd had gone completely silent now, even the wind seeming to hold its breath.

"On three?" Sophie asked.

"On three," they agreed.

Sophie moved to her spot at the base of the tree. The bark was rough under her paws, cold in a way that had nothing to do with temperature. She could feel the wrongness pulsing just beneath the surface, feel the tree dying inch by inch, feel the weight of hundreds of watching eyes pressing down on her shoulders. Morty took his position across from her while Zip hovered at the third point, all three of them forming a triangle around the ancient trunk.

"One," Sophie called out.

She placed the golden berry on the ground and began to dig. Her claws hit earth and immediately she knew something was wrong ... the ground was hard, harder than it should be, packed solid like stone. She dug frantically, but the soil wouldn't give, wouldn't accept what she was trying to plant.

"Two," Morty's voice was already strained.

He was having the same problem, his paws scraping and bleeding as he clawed at the unyielding earth. Without his spectacles working properly ... one lens gone, the other cracked ... he couldn't even see what he was doing, could only feel for depth and softness that refused to materialize. The ground remained hard, impenetrable, like the forest itself was rejecting their offering.

"Three," Zip's voice cracked.

He tried to help dig with his tiny legs, pushing at the earth with all his small strength, but he was too little, too exhausted. His wings trembled with the effort of staying airborne after everything they'd been through. Around them, the crowd began to murmur ... nervous sounds, uncertain whispers that built like a wave.

"It's not working," someone said.

Sophie's claws scraped raw against the packed earth. Pain shot through her paws, sharp and immediate, but she kept digging anyway. Dirt caked under her aching claws, mixing with the small cuts that stung but weren't serious. She could feel the golden berry in her other paw growing dimmer and fainter, its warmth fading like a life slipping away.

Beside her, Morty was gasping with effort, his small paws scraped and aching as he clawed at the unyielding earth. His paws were getting cut up from the rough soil, but he didn't stop. Every scrape against the packed earth sent jolts of discomfort up his arms, but he kept going. Couldn't stop. Behind him, he could hear the crowd's growing doubt ... whispers turning to mutters, hope turning to disappointment.

"The ground's rejecting them," someone said, louder now.

"They're too late," another voice added.

"The magic is already dead."

No. The word roared through Morty's mind. They hadn't survived the fog, the storm, the river, the thicket ... hadn't come all this way ... to fail because of stubborn dirt.

Zip hovered above his spot, his tiny body pushing and scraping and accomplishing almost nothing. His wings were screaming with exhaustion, his light flickering wildly with panic. Below him, the earth looked as solid and unyielding as stone. How was he supposed to dig through that? He was too small, too weak, too ...

"Stop thinking you're not enough!" Sophie's voice cut through his spiral, fierce despite her own pain. "You ARE enough, Zip! We ALL are! We just have to ... "

Her paw punched through the crust.

The sensation was so sudden, so unexpected, Sophie almost lost her balance. One moment she was clawing uselessly at packed earth, the next her paw had broken through into softer soil beneath. The resistance hadn't been the whole way down ... just a barrier. A test.

"There's another layer!" Her voice exploded with hope and urgency. "Keep digging! Don't give up! There's soft earth underneath!"

Morty adjusted his technique immediately, concentrating on feeling rather than seeing, using his underground instincts to search for weaknesses in the packed surface. His sensitive paws detected a slight give near the edge of his hole. He focused there, working the spot, and suddenly ... breakthrough. His paws sank into soil that felt right, that felt like it would accept the seed.

"I'm through too!" he called out, his voice cracking with relief.

Zip redoubled his efforts, his exhausted wings beating faster, his tiny legs pushing with everything he had. The crowd's doubt was getting louder, more certain. He could hear them giving up, could feel their disappointment pressing down on him like physical weight. But Sophie and Morty believed in him. They'd said he was enough.

He had to prove them right.

His tiny body threw itself at the earth with renewed determination, scraping and pushing and refusing to quit even when his muscles screamed and his wings felt like they might tear. And then ... impossibly, miraculously ... he felt it. A tiny crack in the surface. He worked at it, widened it, pushed through, and suddenly he was in softer soil, digging deeper, creating space for the precious seed he'd carried so far.

"I did it!" The words burst out of him, surprised and triumphant. "I'm through!"

The holes were ready. Finally, impossibly, ready.

Sophie lifted the golden berry with trembling, dirt-covered paws. Her paws were scraped and sore from digging, stinging from dozens of small cuts, but none of it mattered now. It was so dim now she could barely feel its warmth anymore, like holding a dying ember that had only seconds left before going cold forever. She brought it close to her chest, whispering to it like she had during the storm. "You've made it this far. We've made it this far. Please don't give up now. Please."

The berry pulsed once ... so faint she almost missed it. Like it heard her. Like it was trying to promise it would keep fighting.

Sophie placed it carefully into the hole, settling it at the bottom with gentle precision, treating it like the most precious thing in the world because right now, it was. Her bloody paws pushed soil over it, packing it down with care and desperation mixed together.

Morty cradled the silver berry in his paws for just a moment, feeling its weak pulse, seeing its flickering light even through his cracked spectacles. "We trusted you to guide us," he whispered to it. "Now trust us to give you a home." He placed it in the hole with movements that were reverent despite his shaking hands and sightless left eye, covering it with earth and hope in equal measure.

Zip used his legs to roll the blue-green berry to the edge of his hole. It was almost as big as his entire body, heavy with fading magic, glowing so dimly it was like looking at a star on the verge of dying. He positioned himself carefully, ready to guide it down ...

And his exhausted wing spasmed.

The berry slipped from his grasp, tumbling into the hole at completely the wrong angle, bouncing off the side, rolling toward the edge where it would fall out completely and probably roll away and be lost forever and this entire quest would fail because he was too weak and too tired and too ...

The crowd gasped. A hundred voices drawing breath as one, the sound like a scream of dismay.

Zip didn't think. His body reacted purely on instinct and desperation. He dove straight down into the hole, wings folding tight, falling like a tiny meteor. The walls of the hole rushed past him. The berry was still rolling, still falling. He stretched his legs out, reached with every part of his tiny body, and ...

Caught it.

His legs wrapped around the berry. His wings exploded open, beating frantically to stop their fall. The hole was narrow, the walls pressing in, but somehow he managed to slow their descent, to control it, to guide the berry down to the soft earth at the bottom where it belonged.

He landed on top of it, breathing hard, his whole body shaking. For a moment he just lay there, sprawled across the blue-green berry in the bottom of the hole, wings trembling, heart hammering, unable to believe he'd actually done that.

Then he heard applause.

Not everyone in the crowd ... just a few animals at first. But those few had seen the catch, had watched this tiny firefly who could barely glow make an impossible save. And the applause spread, growing louder, until the clearing was ringing with it.

Zip looked up from the bottom of the hole to see Sophie and Morty staring down at him with expressions of pure awe and pride.

"That," Sophie said, her voice filled with wonder, "was the most amazing thing I've ever seen."

"That was spectacular," Morty agreed, pushing his spectacles up with shaking paws.

Zip's light blazed brighter than it had in days ... not from magic or external power, but from pure pride and the absolute certainty that he was exactly where he belonged, doing exactly what he was meant to do.

He carefully positioned the berry in the softest part of the soil, treating it with the reverence it deserved. Then he flew out of the hole, his friends helping to cover the berry with earth, all three of them working to pack it down gently but firmly.

Three small mounds at the base of the dying tree. Three seeds buried. Three friends standing side-by-side, bloody and exhausted and trembling with fear and hope.

They stepped back and waited for something ... anything ... to happen.

Nothing did.

The silence that followed was crushing. Sophie stared at the spot where she'd planted the golden berry, her eyes desperately searching for any sign ... a glow, a shimmer, a pulse of light, anything. But the dirt looked completely normal. Just dirt. Just earth. Showing no sign of the magic buried beneath.

Her heart hammered so hard it hurt. She looked at Morty and saw his face had gone pale, his paws clenched into white-knuckled fists. She looked at Zip and saw his light flickering wildly, faster and more erratic than she'd ever seen it, like his body couldn't decide between panic and hope.

The crowd held its collective breath. Every animal frozen, watching, waiting. One second passed, feeling like an eternity. Then another. Then another.

Still nothing.

The mounds of earth remained dark. Lifeless. Just dirt covering what might already be dead magic.

"Did we do it wrong?" Zip's voice was barely a whisper, breaking with emotion he couldn't contain.

Morty's paws dug into the earth beside his mound, checking, searching with increasingly frantic movements. "They're planted correctly. Deep enough. The right spots. Three points of a triangle. It should be working. It should ... "

Five seconds. Six. Seven.

The crowd's silence was starting to crack. Sophie could hear it ... the shift from hopeful waiting to disappointed acceptance. Small sounds. Shuffling feet. Whispered words that cut like knives.

"It didn't work," someone said, loud enough for everyone to hear.

The words hit Sophie like a physical blow, stealing the breath from her lungs. Her legs wanted to run, to escape all these watching eyes and disappointed faces. Every instinct screamed at her to bolt, to hide, to get away from the crushing weight of failure pressing down on her chest.

She could feel her parents leaving again ... could see them walking away without looking back, could hear her own small voice asking "Can I come?" and getting nothing but silence in return. Could feel every single moment of not-enough, not-ready, not-worth-keeping catching up with her all at once in this terrible, stretched-out present.

"No," she whispered, the word barely more than an exhaled breath. "Please, no. We did everything right. We came so far. Please."

Eight seconds. Nine. Ten.

Morty's scientific mind was racing, cataloging possibilities, searching desperately for what they'd missed. Wrong depth? Wrong spacing? Wrong alignment with the tree? But everything was correct, everything was exactly as the ancient texts had described, so why wasn't it ...

The crowd began to shift with subtle movements that spoke louder than words. Animals starting to turn away, parents pulling children closer in preparation to leave, the collective body language of a crowd accepting disappointment.

Someone actually started walking away, and others followed, and Sophie wanted to scream at them to wait, to give it more time, but what if there was no more time? What if they really had failed?

This was it, then. The end. Three small animals who'd tried their absolute hardest and discovered... sometimes your best isn't enough. Sometimes courage and determination and friendship can't overcome reality. That sometimes ...

Then, **the berries flared.**

Not gradually. Not with warning or buildup or any chance to prepare. The light exploded from beneath the earth with such sudden, violent force Sophie actually stumbled backward, her paws leaving the ground for a second.

This wasn't the gentle glow they'd carried from the grove, wasn't the weak flicker they'd nursed through storm and fog and desperate miles. This was *power* ... raw and ancient and overwhelming, blazing up from the three planting spots in columns of silver and gold and blue-green light so bright they hurt to look at directly, so intense animals in the front of the crowd had to shield their eyes.

The light was alive. Sophie's first coherent thought as the initial shock wore off. The light was alive and joyful and singing, pouring out of the earth like it had been trapped for centuries and was finally, gloriously free.

Sophie felt it before she fully understood what was happening ... a shock ran through her bones like electricity, through her chest like thunder, through her injured leg with such intense burning heat she cried out in pain and surprise. Then the burning transformed, became something else entirely, became healing flowing through her like liquid sunlight. The old wound from the climbing challenge ... the one that had throbbed and ached through the entire journey home ... suddenly blazed with warmth. She felt the scar tissue underneath her fur melting away like ice in sunshine, felt the damaged muscle knitting back together, felt the deep ache that had become so constant she'd stopped noticing it finally, blessedly disappear.

The sound came next ... like thunder and singing and bells all at once, like every musical note ever played happening simultaneously, so loud she couldn't think, could only feel the vibrations running through every part of her body, making her teeth rattle and her bones hum in harmony with the tree's awakening.

Morty tore off his broken spectacles because suddenly ... impossibly ... he didn't need them. His left eye, which had been seeing nothing but blur since the lens broke, could suddenly see clearly. Perfectly. Better than it ever had before, even with the spectacles. The tree was blazing before him with light so bright it should have been painful but somehow wasn't, and he could make out every single detail with crystalline clarity ... every branch, every returning starberry, every animal's expression of shocked wonder.

He looked down at his spectacles in his paw. The cracked lens was still cracked. But his eyes didn't need them anymore. The tree's magic had somehow fixed what the water had broken.

Zip's light exploded in response to the tree's awakening, synchronizing with the massive surge of magic in a way that made his whole tiny body pulse with the same rhythm as the starberries erupting on every branch above them. He was glowing brighter than he'd ever glowed in his entire life ... brighter than his siblings, brighter than his parents, brighter than he'd ever imagined possible. His small form blazed like a captured star, and for the first time in his life, Zip understood that bright wasn't about comparison. Bright was about purpose. And right now, his purpose was to be part of this miracle.

The light hit the tree trunk and spread with impossible speed, racing up the bark in spiraling patterns that looked almost like staircases or rivers or roads leading to the sky. Where the light touched, the bark smoothed and strengthened, cracks sealing themselves with audible snapping sounds, decay reversing so fast you could actually watch it happen.

The wrongness that had been spreading from the roots withered and died, pushed back by pure magic, dissolved like shadows in sunlight.

Branches that had hung limp and brittle straightened and reached upward as if suddenly remembering how to be alive, remembering what it felt like to be strong and healthy and full of sap and life. New growth burst from old wood ... leaves unfurling, buds forming, the whole tree coming alive in a matter of seconds like someone had pressed fast-forward on spring itself.

The smell changed too ... the acrid stench of decay and endings replaced by something that smelled like spring mornings and new growth and petrichor after rain and magic itself made manifest in the physical world. It smelled like hope, if hope had a scent.

The whispers came back.

Soft at first, like a distant voice calling from far away. Then stronger, clearer, building in volume and complexity. Then overwhelming ... the familiar hum that had always been there, the song of the tree, the heartbeat of the forest returning with such force that every animal in the clearing could feel it wrapping around them like an embrace from someone they'd thought they'd lost forever.

Like coming home after being lost for so long they'd forgotten what home felt like. Like remembering something precious they'd thought was gone forever but had only been sleeping, waiting patiently for someone brave enough and desperate enough and loving enough to wake it.

The whispers sang of memory and gratitude and welcome. They sang of ancient days and future hopes. They sang of three small heroes who'd done what no one thought possible.

Sophie felt tears streaming down her face ... hot against her fur, falling freely ... and she didn't even try to stop them or hide them or pretend she wasn't completely overwhelmed.

Beside her, Morty had abandoned his spectacles completely and was wiping his eyes with shaking paws, and she could see he was crying too, the stoic mole who planned everything finally letting emotion break through his careful control.

Zip's light blazed and pulsed above them, so bright it cast sharp shadows even in the tree's overwhelming radiance, and she could see his tiny body shaking with what looked like joy and relief and disbelief all mixed as one.

And then ... impossibly, beautifully, magnificently ... the starberries began to grow.

Not just the three they'd planted, but all of them, the entire tree erupting in thousands upon thousands of glowing points of light. Each one was a perfect star-shaped berry that grew from nothing to full size in seconds, brightening as it matured until the Starberry Tree looked exactly like its name ... like someone had captured an entire night sky full of stars and woven them into branches, like the boundary between earth and heaven had blurred and melte into something that belonged to both and neither.

The light was overwhelming in the best possible way, pushing back the approaching night and filling the clearing with radiance so pure and complete that every animal standing there felt it in their bones, in their hearts, in the deepest parts of themselves that remembered what wonder felt like before the world taught them to be jaded and careful.

The ground beneath their feet shook ... not violently or dangerously, but rhythmically, purposefully, like a massive heart starting to beat again after being still for too long. Like the tree's roots were stretching deep into the earth and finding joy there. Like the whole forest was waking up and remembering what it meant to be alive.

This was what the forest had been missing, what home was supposed to feel like ... this sense of rightness, of completion, of everything being exactly where it belonged and doing exactly what it was meant to do.

The crowd erupted into chaos.

Not just cheering but something wilder, more primal ... animals who'd been strangers moments before were rushing forward, embracing each other, crying and laughing and celebrating with complete abandon.

The young squirrel Sophie would meet later came charging through the crowd like a furry missile and tackled her in a hug so enthusiastic it knocked her completely flat on her back. Birds dove from the branches with flower petals clutched in their beaks, scattering them over everything like the most beautiful, chaotic storm.

Even the normally dignified deer were jumping and spinning like they'd forgotten they were supposed to be graceful and composed, their usual composure completely forgotten in the face of such overwhelming joy.

The badger's granddaughter emerged from her burrow for the first time in months, blinking in the brilliant light that flooded even into underground spaces. Her face showed pure wonder instead of the fear that had kept her hidden for so long, and when she saw Sophie watching, she waved ... actually waved ... with a shy but genuine smile.

Old enemies forgot their grudges. Prey animals danced with predators. The most ancient creatures in the forest wept openly, remembering days when the tree had been young and they had been younger. Parents lifted their children high so they could see better, and the little ones squealed with delight at all the pretty lights.

But Sophie barely registered the celebration swirling around her, too focused on the tree itself, on the miracle they'd created. She was staring upward at the glowing branches, at the thousands of starberries pulsing in perfect rhythm like a single living heartbeat spread across infinite points of light, and feeling something crack open in her chest ... something which had been closed tight and locked away for so long she'd forgotten it was there.

That voice had whispered "not enough" every day since her parents left. The certainty she needed to be spectacular and perfect and impressive to matter. The fear that if she wasn't the fastest and the bravest and the best, no one would remember her name or care she'd existed.

All of it ... gone. Dissolved in the light of a simple, impossible truth: She had mattered. Not because she was the most spectacular squirrel in the forest, but because when her home needed her, she'd shown up. She'd tried. She'd broken and healed and kept going.

And that was enough. She was enough. Had always been enough.

"We did it," Morty breathed beside her, his voice filled with wonder and disbelief.

"We saved the tree," Zip added, his light still blazing with unprecedented brightness.

"We saved home," Sophie whispered, and somehow it felt like the most important truth of all.

Ophelia landed beside them, her ancient face wet with tears she made no attempt to hide. Her voice cracked when she spoke, all her usual composure and wisdom stripped away to reveal raw emotion underneath. "Thank you. Thank you for giving me back my family."

The crowd was surging forward now, everyone wanting to thank them, to touch them, to celebrate with the heroes who'd saved the forest. But before the animals could reach them, something else happened that made even the celebration pause.

The tree pulsed.

Once. Twice. Three times. Four, five, six, seven ... a rhythmic pulsing that seemed to resonate in everyone's chest, matching their heartbeats, synchronizing with their breathing, creating a moment of perfect unity between every living thing in the clearing.

And then, from the trunk itself, light began to gather and coalesce, pulling together from the surrounding radiance, taking shape, forming into something that looked almost like figures ... animal-like but larger, more majestic, proportioned in ways that didn't quite match any living species, made entirely of starlight and magic and ancient memory given temporary form.

The ancient ones.

Or their memory, at least. Their echo in the magic they'd planted three hundred years ago, preserved somehow in the tree's essence and called forth by this moment of awakening. The clearing went silent again as every animal fell to their knees or bowed their heads or lowered themselves in whatever gesture of reverence came naturally to their species. Even Ophelia, ancient and wise and powerful in her own right, lowered herself respectfully before these beings of pure magic.

But the starlight figures weren't looking at the crowd. They were looking at Sophie, Morty, and Zip with eyes that seemed to see past flesh and fur into something deeper ... into the journey they'd taken, the changes they'd undergone, the truth of who they'd become through trial and struggle and the choice to keep going even when stopping would have been easier.

One figure ... wolf-shaped with wise eyes holding centuries of knowledge ... stepped forward, and its voice was like wind through trees, like water over stone, like the whispers themselves given form and speech and purpose:

"You have done what we hoped would never be necessary. The tree thanks you. The forest thanks you. And we thank you."

Sophie found her voice despite the trembling in her legs and the overwhelming weight of being addressed by beings of pure magic. "We just did what anyone would do." Even as she said it, she knew it wasn't quite true ... not anyone would have kept going through fog and storm and fear and doubt, but it felt wrong somehow to claim they were special or chosen or anything other than three scared animals who'd tried their best.

The wolf-figure's eyes glowed warmer, and somehow Sophie knew it was pleased with her answer rather than disappointed by her humility.

"No. You did what only you could do. Three who were broken found each other. Three who were lost found home. Three who were separate became one."

It turned to Morty, and its gaze seemed to pierce right through him, seeing every moment of doubt and every act of courage with equal clarity. *"You learned that wisdom without courage is only fear dressed in clever words."*

Morty's paw went to his spectacles automatically, then stopped when he remembered he didn't need them anymore, that he could see clearly now in more ways than one.

The wolf-figure turned to Zip next, and its voice gentled somehow, became even more tender. *"You learned that the smallest light can banish the deepest darkness."* Zip's glow pulsed brighter in response, no longer dimmed by shame or inadequacy but blazing with the certainty of his own worth.

Finally it turned to Sophie, and she felt its gaze settle on her like a warm weight, heavy but not crushing. *"You learned true strength comes not from being unbreakable, but from being willing to break and heal together."*

The words hit Sophie hard because they were true ... she'd spent so long trying to be unbreakable, trying to prove she didn't need anyone, and learning to need her friends had been harder than any physical challenge she'd faced.

The three friends looked at each other, overwhelmed and changed and somehow still themselves despite everything that had happened to them.

The wolf-figure continued, and its voice seemed to resonate not just in their ears but in their chests, in their bones, in the deepest parts of themselves: *"You planted three berries. But you grew something else. Something more precious. You grew understanding. You grew trust. You grew love."*

The starlight figures began to fade, their purpose fulfilled, their message delivered, dissolving back into the light they'd been shaped from.

The wolf-figure spoke one last time, its voice growing fainter as it returned to wherever such beings went when they weren't needed anymore:

"The tree will remember you. The forest will remember you. And when you are old and gray and your own children ask about heroes, you will tell them: heroes are not the ones who are never afraid. Heroes are the ones who are terrified and do it anyway."

And then they were gone, dissolving back into light, back into the tree, back into the magic they'd left behind centuries ago as a gift for generations they'd never meet but had trusted would rise to meet whatever challenges came.

For a moment, no one moved or spoke, the weight of what they'd witnessed still pressing down on the clearing. Then the crowd surged forward again, and this time there was no stopping them, no pause for more magic or more messages.

Animals surrounded Sophie, Morty, and Zip completely, thanking them and celebrating them and lifting them up on shoulders and wings and antlers, carrying them through the crowd like the heroes they'd become despite never setting out to be anything other than three scared animals trying to save something they loved.

Sophie caught Morty's eye across the celebration and saw him grinning ... actually grinning, something she'd rarely seen him do back when they'd first met and he'd been nothing but anxiety and careful planning.

Zip was being carefully passed from animal to animal, his light blazing with joy and pride and the kind of belonging he'd never felt before, each creature treating him with gentle reverence despite his small size. They'd done it. They'd actually, truly, impossibly done it.

The celebration continued long into the night, showing no signs of slowing down despite the late hour. The Starberry Tree glowed overhead with such brilliance it turned night into day, its light reaching far beyond the clearing to illuminate the entire forest. Its whispers sang loud and joyful enough every animal in Thistlewood could hear them, could feel the music wrapping around them like a promise everything would be all right now, that the darkness was over, home was safe again.

And beneath its branches, three unlikely heroes ... a mole, a squirrel, and a firefly ... sat together, finally allowed to rest, watching the lights dance in the branches above them and knowing they'd changed the world. But more importantly, much more importantly, they'd changed each other, had learned what it meant to be a team, had discovered the greatest magic wasn't in ancient berries or glowing trees but in the simple, the *powerful act of choosing to face impossible things, together rather than alone. Believing in oneself and others.*

***that* was the greatest magic of all.**

CHAPTER TWELVE

Home

The celebration beneath the Starberry Tree lasted until the stars themselves came out to watch.

Animals who'd been strangers that morning were friends by evening. The normally grumpy badgers were dancing ... actually dancing ... with the rabbits. Birds sang from the glowing branches. Even the deer, who prided themselves on dignity, were jumping and spinning with joy.

Sophie sat on a low branch, watching it all, still not quite believing it was real. The tree glowed above her, each starberry a point of light against the darkening sky. The whispers hummed gently, wrapping around every animal like a warm blanket. Everything was exactly as it should be.

Except for the small voice in her head asking: Now what?

"There you are!" A gruff voice interrupted her thoughts.

She looked down to see the oldest badger in the forest ... the one who never smiled, never spoke to anyone, was always grumbling about noise and nonsense. He was holding something in his paws.

A single white flower.

"My granddaughter has been hiding in the burrow for months," he said, not quite meeting Sophie's eyes. "Too scared to come out. Says she's not brave enough for the world." He looked up, and his eyes were wet. "But tonight, she watched you three plant those berries. Watched you stand there, scared but doing it anyway. And she turned to me and said, 'If they can be brave, maybe I can too.' She picked this for you. Asked me to say thank you. For showing her that brave doesn't mean not scared."

Sophie took the flower with trembling paws, unsure what to say. The badger nodded once and walked away, leaving her staring at the flower and feeling something warm expand in her chest.

She'd wanted to be remembered. To matter. To be special.

But this ... knowing she'd helped one scared little badger find courage ... this felt bigger than any spectacular climb or dangerous stunt ever had.

"Sophie!" Morty called from below. "Come down! Someone wants to meet you!"

She climbed down to find a young squirrel waiting nervously, barely old enough to have left his mother's nest. The young squirrel's tail twitched with anxiety as he explained he'd heard Sophie was the fastest climber in the forest and wanted to learn from her.

Old Sophie would have puffed up with pride. Would have immediately demonstrated her most impressive moves. Would have made it about showing off.

New Sophie knelt down to the young squirrel's level. "Climbing isn't about being the fastest," she said gently. "It's about being patient. Careful. Thinking through each move before you make it. My friend Morty taught me that, and it saved my life."

The young squirrel's eyes went wide. "Really? But everyone says you're so fast and brave and ... "

"I am fast. But I'm only alive because I learned to slow down." Sophie gestured to Morty. "This is the bravest animal I know. And the smartest. If you want to learn to climb, he should teach you as much as I do."

Morty's eyes went suspiciously shiny behind his cracked spectacles.

Across the clearing, Zip was having his own moment. A firefly had approached ... young, light dim and flickering with anxiety.

"I wish I glowed like the others," the young firefly whispered, so quietly Zip almost didn't hear. "Everyone says I'm too dim. That I'll never be bright enough to matter."

Zip's light pulsed ... steady, certain, exactly the brightness it needed to be. "I used to think the same thing. Spent my whole life wishing I was brighter. But you know what I learned? Being bright like others isn't the point. Being bright like YOU is the point. The world doesn't need another copy of someone else's light. It needs yours. *Exactly as it is.*" He let that sink in for a moment. "Your light is perfect. Trust me ... I spent days in the dark learning the lesson."

The young firefly's glow strengthened just a little. Just enough.

As the celebration continued, Morty found himself pulled away from the noise. Something was nagging at him. Had been nagging at him since the tree lit up.

He walked to the trunk, to the carved symbols covering the ancient bark. They were glowing now ... had been glowing since the moment the starberries took root. Silver-white light traced each spiral, each curve, each mysterious mark.

But one symbol was different.

It was new ... Morty was certain of it. He'd studied these symbols for days before they left on the quest. He knew every mark, every pattern. And this one hadn't been there before.

It glowed red instead of silver. Pulsed with urgent rhythm. And it was counting down.

Seven marks within the symbol. Six were dark. One was lit.

Morty's paws trembled as he traced it. He didn't know what it meant. But every instinct he had ... every underground sense, every planning-obsessed part of his brain ... was screaming that this was important.

"You noticed it too." Ophelia's voice came from behind him, her ancient eyes fixed on the symbol.

Morty turned to face her, his paw still on the glowing mark. "What is it?"

"A warning. Or a summons. Perhaps both." Ophelia landed on a lower branch, her gaze never leaving the red glow. "Did you count the pulses? When the tree awoke?"

Morty nodded slowly. "Seven. There were exactly seven."

"The old texts speak of Seven Groves," Ophelia said, as if remembering something from a very long time ago. "Seven trees planted by the ancient ones across the world. When one awakens, it calls to the others." She paused, and Morty saw something like fear flicker in her ancient eyes. "You didn't just save Thistlewood. You woke them all. Every tree. Every grove.

You announced to everything magical in the world that the age of starlight has begun again."

Morty felt his stomach drop. "And is that bad?"

Ophelia's silence was answer enough. When she finally spoke, her voice was heavy with concern. "The light returned. And in returning, it sent out a signal like a beacon. To friends, yes. But also to enemies. To things that have been sleeping. Waiting. Things that remember the age of starlight ... and the war that ended it."

A cold feeling settled in Morty's chest. He wanted to ask what she meant, what war, what enemies. But Ophelia looked at him with eyes both proud and sad. "You've changed, young Morty. All of you have. You're ready for what's next."

"What if we're not?"

"You will be. You always were." She flew back toward the celebration, leaving Morty alone with the glowing countdown.

One lit. Six dark.

He turned to walk back to his friends ... and froze.

Something was wrong with the shadows.

Just for a moment. Just long enough to notice. That deer over there ... its shadow moved when it didn't. That rabbit laughing by the food ... its shadow stretched too long, reached too far, moved in ways shadows shouldn't move.

Morty blinked. The shadows were normal again.

Had he imagined it?

(He hadn't. But he wanted to believe he had.)

As the celebration finally began to wind down, as exhausted animals started drifting toward home with full bellies and happy hearts, the three friends found themselves alone at the base of the tree.

Above them, the Starberry Tree glowed with thousands of lights. The whispers sang softly, contentedly. Everything looked peaceful.

Sophie leaned against the trunk, the white flower still in her paw, her eyes distant. Morty settled beside her, adjusting his cracked spectacles, and asked what she was thinking about.

Sophie was quiet for a moment, watching the last few animals drift away into the forest. "Just wondering what happens next. We did it ... we finished the quest. We saved the tree. And now..." She spread her paws helplessly. "Now what?"

Before anyone could answer, the tree pulsed.

Once. Twice. Three times. Four, five, six, seven.

And then, from high in the branches, three starberries fell.

Not the magical ones they'd planted. Regular ones. But as they fell, they glowed ... changing color as they dropped, transforming into something else.

They landed softly in front of the three friends.

Sophie's berry burned gold like courage made solid.

Morty's shimmered silver like wisdom given form.

Zip's pulsed soft blue like hope made real.

"The tree remembers," Ophelia said softly, appearing beside them. "It gifts its saviors. Keep them. You'll need them for the next journey."

Zip's voice was small and uncertain. "Next journey?"

Ophelia looked at the horizon, at the darkening sky. "This was only the beginning."

They sat with their gifts, with their tree, with each other. The celebration had ended. The other animals had gone home. It was just the three of them now, and the glowing tree, and the night full of stars.

Sophie tucked the golden berry into her fur, feeling its warmth pulse against her chest. "I'm tired," she admitted. "Bone-deep, fall-asleep-standing-up tired."

Zip's light dimmed to a soft glow. "Me too. I don't think I've ever been this exhausted in my entire life."

Morty pulled blankets from his seemingly endless satchel, already arranging them against the tree trunk. "Let's stay here tonight. Under the tree."

They didn't need to discuss it. They simply settled against the trunk, wrapped in blankets, the three of them close enough to feel each other breathing.

For a while, they just sat there in comfortable silence, watching the stars emerge one by one, listening to the whispers, feeling the weight of everything they'd accomplished settling over them like a warm blanket.

Sophie broke the silence first, her voice quiet in the darkness. "Zip? That night. During the celebration. Did you see... did the shadows look wrong to you? Like they were moving on their own?"

A long pause. Then Zip's voice came, barely above a whisper. "Yes. I thought I imagined it. Thought maybe I was just so exhausted my eyes were playing tricks."

Morty shifted beside them, his voice thoughtful. "I saw it too. Just for a moment. That deer's shadow moved when it shouldn't have. And that rabbit ... its shadow stretched in ways that didn't make sense."

They lay there in silence, processing this. All three of them had seen it. Which meant it hadn't been exhaustion or imagination or fear. Something had been there. Something did move in the shadows and watched from darkness.

Zip's voice trembled slightly when he spoke again. "Should we be worried?"

Morty considered this carefully. "Maybe. But not tonight. Tonight we're safe. The tree is here. Whatever that was, it's not here now."

Sophie felt for her friends' paws in the darkness, found them, held on tight. "And if it comes back? If whatever that was shows up when we're not ready?"

"Then we'll face it," Morty said simply, squeezing back. "Same way we faced everything else. We'll figure it out together."

Sophie's voice was steady despite the fear curling in her stomach. "Together."

Zip's light pulsed once, soft and certain. "Always together."

Above them, the Starberry Tree's whispers grew gentler, like a lullaby, like the forest itself was tucking them in.

Sleep now, little heroes, the whispers seemed to say. *You've earned your rest. The light is home. The magic is restored. And you ... you three ... are exactly where you belong.*

Tomorrow brings new questions. New mysteries. New paths to walk.

But tonight, you are home.

And that is enough.

Sophie drifted off first, the golden berry warm against her chest, her paws still holding tight to her friends. Zip followed soon after, his light dimming to almost nothing but never quite going out, his small body nestled safely between Sophie and Morty. Morty stayed awake the longest, his mind already working on the countdown symbol, on the Seven Groves, on what it all meant.

But eventually, even Morty slept, wrapped in warmth and friendship and the absolute certainty whatever came next, they'd face it.

One week later, Morty's tunnel smelled like heaven.

Earthy mushrooms simmered with wild thyme, a hint of garlic, and something Morty called his "secret ingredient" that tasted like sunshine and butter and home all mixed together. Fresh bread ... actually BAKED bread ... sat cooling on a stone shelf, its crust golden-brown and crackling softly.

"This is amazing," Sophie said, savoring every bite. "Seriously, Morty. You could open a restaurant."

"A restaurant requires dealing with the public," Morty replied, stirring the pot. "Which sounds terrible. I'll stick to cooking for friends."

"Perfect choice," Zip added from his mushroom-cap seat, his light casting warm shadows across the walls.

Life had settled into something wonderful. Not the same as before ... better. Sophie still did her morning workouts, but now she invited others to join. Morty still organized his maps and research, but his tunnel didn't feel lonely anymore because friends visited almost every day. And Zip, who'd once hidden in the shadows, now glowed steadily in his cozy home within the Starberry Tree itself, finally certain that he belonged.

On Morty's desk, beside the lamp, sat three small objects that pulsed with soft light.

The gift berries.

Gold for courage. Silver for wisdom. Blue for hope.

"Have they done anything?" Sophie asked, nodding toward them. "Since that first night?"

"Just glow," Morty admitted. "Waiting, I think. For when they're needed." He adjusted his cracked spectacles. "I've been researching. The Seven Groves. The countdown. What it all means."

"And?" Zip prompted.

"And I think we'll know when the time comes." Morty smiled. "But not today. Today we just get to be with each other. Tomorrow we explore the northern ridge. Next week, who knows? Maybe we'll find another small adventure. Something low-stakes and fun."

"And someday," Sophie said quietly, looking at the glowing berries, "when those six other groves need help ... "

"We'll go," Zip finished, his light steady.

"together, always" Morty agreed with a confident smile.

They ate in comfortable silence, the kind which only exists between people completely at ease with each other. Outside, evening sounds filtered through ... birds settling, wind rustling leaves, the distant whispers of the Starberry Tree singing its eternal song.

After dinner, they walked outside. The night was clear and cool, stars scattered across the sky. The Starberry Tree glowed in the distance, its lights pulsing gently.

"Beautiful," Zip breathed.

"It really is," Sophie agreed. She touched the golden berry in her pocket, feeling its warmth. "Hard to believe it was dark just a week ago."

"Hard to believe we're the ones who saved it," Morty added quietly.

They stood together in the peaceful darkness, three unlikely friends who'd become unlikely heroes. Tomorrow would bring small adventures. Someday would bring bigger ones. But tonight, they were exactly where they needed to be.

Home.

The Starberry Tree glowed through the night, its whispers singing of journeys completed and journeys yet to come.

And far away, in forests they'd never seen, in groves they'd never visited, six trees stood dark and silent.

Waiting.

Not forever. Just until the heroes were ready.

In Thistlewood Forest, the countdown symbol pulsed once.

One lit. Six dark.

The first star was shining. Five more would need their light.

But that was a story for another day.

Tonight, three heroes ... a squirrel, a mole, and a firefly ... were home, safe, and exactly where they belonged.

And in those dreams, the gift berries pulsed softly ... gold and silver and blue, waiting patiently for the day they'd be needed again.

For the day when the call would come. The day when three unlikely heroes would answer.

Together. Because....

“Sometimes the greatest magic is believing in yourself...and others”

THE END ... *but only for now, this is just the beginning of many adventures to come... with more new friends, perils and excitement along the way. Please join us, it will be fun.*

The Starberry Fantasy Adventure Series

W & G Coakley

MEET THE HEROES

MORTY: The Worrier Who Found Courage

NAME: Mortimer (but everyone calls him Morty)

SPECIES: Mole | AGE: 8 years old

HOME: An organized tunnel network beneath the oak grove, with exactly three entrance points (one might get blocked, two might not be enough, four would be excessive)

APPEARANCE: Small with velvety gray-brown fur, a sensitive pink nose, and thick quartz spectacles that fog up at inconvenient moments

PERSONALITY: Anxious, meticulous, brilliant, and loyal. Morty worries about everything, but that careful nature makes him an excellent planner and navigator.

SPECIAL SKILLS: Underground navigation in complete darkness • Ancient language translation • Organized packing • Staying calm in a crisis (after panicking first)

BIGGEST FEAR: Making a mistake that puts his friends in danger

WHAT HE LEARNED: Being brave doesn't mean not being scared ... it means trusting yourself even when you can't see the way forward.

FUN FACT: Morty once spent three hours organizing his emergency acorn supply alphabetically, then realized acorns don't have names.

SOPHIE: The Performer Who Found Patience

NAME: Sophia Sue , everyone calls her Sophie

SPECIES: Squirrel | AGE: 9 years old

HOME: A nest in the high branches of an ancient oak, chosen for its impressive view and skill to reach it.

APPEARANCE: Sleek reddish-brown fur with a magnificent, fluffy tail. Quick, graceful movements and bright eyes always looking for the next challenge

PERSONALITY: Confident, athletic, impulsive, and fiercely loyal. Sophie spent years trying to prove she was spectacular, but learned that true strength comes from slowing down and putting others first.

SPECIAL SKILLS: Climbing anything vertical • Incredible jumping and acrobatics • Quick reflexes • Encouraging others when they doubt themselves

BIGGEST FEAR: Being left behind or forgotten

WHAT SHE LEARNED: Being impressive isn't the same as being brave, and slowing down isn't weakness ... it's wisdom. She was always enough, even before she proved it.

FUN FACT: Sophie once did seventeen backflips in a row just to see if she could. She got dizzy and had to lie down for an hour.

ZIP : The Dim Light Who Learned to Shine

NAME: Zip... he never knew his real name, they just call him Zip because he is so fast.

SPECIES: Firefly | AGE: Young adult

HOME: A cozy hollow within the Starberry Tree, decorated with soft dandelion fluff.

APPEARANCE: Tiny, even for a firefly, with delicate wings and a light dimmer than most of his kind. But that small light burns steady and true when it matters most.

PERSONALITY: Anxious, gentle, observant, and surprisingly brave. Zip spent his life thinking he was too small and dim to matter, but discovered that even the smallest light can push back the deepest darkness.

SPECIAL SKILLS: Flying through tight spaces • Noticing details everyone misses • Navigating in complete darkness • Making peace between arguing friends • grows brighter when protecting those he loves

BIGGEST FEAR: Being useless, forgotten, or too small

WHAT HE LEARNED: His small light is exactly enough. Being found is sometimes braver than hiding. Worthiness isn't about being the brightest.

FUN FACT: Zip once categorized all his fears by probability and severity, inspired by Morty. "Getting stuck in a spider web" ranked surprisingly high on both.

OPHELIA: The Ancient Guardian

SPECIES: Owl | AGE: Very old (she stopped counting after her hundredth winter)

HOME: The highest branches of the Starberry Tree.

APPEARANCE: Moonlight-colored feathers that shimmer silver in starlight, with ancient amber eyes. Her presence commands respect.

PERSONALITY: Wise, patient, caring, and occasionally cryptic. Ophelia understands that the best guidance comes in questions rather than answers.

SPECIAL SKILLS: Reading old languages • Understanding the tree's whispers and magic • Seeing potential in others before they see it themselves • Silent flight and exceptional night vision

HISTORY: Fifty winters ago, Ophelia arrived at the Starberry Tree alone and lost. The tree became her only family. When it began dying, she faced losing her home.

WHAT SHE KNOWS: The mightiest rivers start as tiny streams, and sometimes the least likely heroes are exactly the ones the world needs most.

FUN FACT: Ophelia has witnessed every major event in Thistlewood Forest for half a century, including the day a young squirrel tried to climb the Starberry Tree in a thunderstorm.

THORNBACK: The Guardian Who Judges Worth

SPECIES: Grizzly Bear | AGE: Ancient (forty winters as guardian)

HOME: The sacred starberry grove deep in the Deep Forest, where seven starberry bushes grow in protected isolation

APPEARANCE: Massive with thick dark brown fur showing silver streaks from age, fierce amber eyes reflecting ancient wisdom, powerful shoulders, battle scars from decades of defending the grove

PERSONALITY: Stern, patient, wise, and fiercely protective. Thornback judges not by strength or perfection, but by honesty, growth, and courage to admit weakness. Intimidating by design but fair in judgment.

SPECIAL SKILLS: Guardian of ancient magic • Judge of worthiness • Protector of sacred places • Seeing truth in others

BIGGEST RESPONSIBILITY: Ensuring the starberries only go to those who have earned them through genuine growth, not just bravery

WHAT HE KNOWS: True worthiness isn't about being perfect ... it's about choosing to be better and grow despite your flaws.

FUN FACT: Thornback turned away hundreds of seekers over forty winters, but when he saw three strangers choose humility over pride, he knew they were the ones.

A NOTE FROM MORTY

Thank you for joining us on our first exciting adventure! If you're wondering whether the story continues ... **it absolutely does.**

Long ago, the ancient ones planted many magical groves across the world. One was just saved. Can the others be saved?

More exciting mystical fantasy adventures wait in the unknown. It won't be an easy journey. We have a lot to overcome, accomplish, experience, and learn. Lots of new and exciting friends. **Lots of magic, mysteries, tests, trials, excitement... and most of all, FUN.**

We look forward to you joining us. We will need your help.

ABOUT THE AUTHORS

W & G Coakley are William and Gayle—husband and wife, but more importantly, partners, best friends, and a team in every adventure. As kids growing up, they were constantly lost in worlds of fantasy and challenging quests—creating maps to imaginary kingdoms, building forts in hidden corners, and spinning tales of heroes who were small but brave. They never really stopped.

A lifelong passion for great storytelling, a deep love for animals of every kind, and an irresistible urge to explore the unknown, they've spent years venturing into hidden places of mystery, solving puzzles, and going where others often don't dare. Their love of the discovering magic in unexpected places inspired **The Starberry Fantasy Adventure Series**.

Having traveled extensively to many places in the world, William and Gayle now call the Southwestern United States home, where they live surrounded by family, friends, and multiple pets. They write for "the young at heart", of any and all ages. They believe the best adventures are the ones we can share, no matter our age.

Before the Last Light Fades is their first *published* work together, but certainly not their last.

Thanks for Reading.
Wishing You Many Blessings

William & Gayle Coakley

www.ingramcontent.com/pod-product-compliance
Lightning Source LLC
LaVergne TN
LVHW020714110826
845149LV00012B/2257

* 9 7 9 8 9 9 3 8 4 9 3 1 7 *